THE HUSTLER

BOSTON HAWKS HOCKEY
BOOK 8

GINA AZZI

THREE CITIES PUBLISHING LLC

The Hustler

Copyright © 2021 by Gina Azzi

ISBN: 978-1-954470-17-0

PROLOGUE

SOFIA

One Month Earlier

"It's not you, it's me," Don says, gripping my hand with the pressure of a limp noodle. I don't know why that stands out to me, but it does. It's silly really because he's not looking me in the eye and he just delivered one of the most cliché breakup excuses of all time and still…I'm annoyed that he's not gripping my fingers when he says it. It's as if his hold, or lack thereof, is telling of the kind of non-relationship we now have.

"Don, we're supposed to get married in five months," I remind him, my voice much too calm for the blow he's delivering. My body has locked down, a cold drip of disbelief trickling down my spine. My stomach is looped in weaver's knots, the kind my mom would knit while sitting at my hospital bedside, hours on end. My heart rattles painfully, a sudden stop followed by a dramatic lurch that makes me nauseous.

I take stock of my physical reactions to the news and yet, my mind clearly hasn't caught up. Because when I open my mouth again, the most ridiculous thing pops out. "I have a dress fitting in six weeks."

Don's expression twists, his eyes filled with a pity I'm familiar with. I haven't seen it in years, having beaten my childhood cancer at the age of twelve, but I'd recognize it anywhere. Seeing it now, on his face, somehow hurts more than his calling off our wedding.

He pities me. Me. The survivor, the believer in magic and miracles, the woman without a day to waste. Me, the woman he was planning to marry until…when? What happened?

His response causes a swell of anger to spout in the pit of my stomach. Am I really going to let another person dictate my future happiness? Erase the dream of a family I was mentally painting in my mind? How dare he?

Ooh, that's good. Anger is something I understand. It's something I know how to channel. It's not something I like leaning into, but in this moment, anger feels safer than numbness. Healthier.

"Don, are you fucking kidding me? I don't understand." My voice rises several octaves, a shake at the end of my words. "What, what happened between yesterday and today? I thought we were planning for a future. A family!"

"A family? Like…kids?" He looks confused, which makes my anger soar into fury.

"Of course, kids! We were planning to get married. Why are you ending us?"

Don shakes his head, dropping my hand completely to wipe it down his face. "Sofia," he sighs, "when we met, well, we rushed into things. We barely know each other."

"We've been engaged for eight months!" I holler. While several of my sorority sisters took longer than that just to *plan* their weddings, this has been my longest romantic relationship to date. After two months, I was ready to marry Don. "Almost a year, Don. I moved to Maui to be with you. I left college, I left my volunteer work, I left my life behind to support your career here, with the understanding that we were starting a life together. A fa-family." I stutter on the last word, feeling my heart snap as I say it. I want to grow a family.

For one blink, Don has the decency to look ashamed. But then he locks his expression down and a detachment I didn't think he was capable of washes over his face. "Family, Sofia? You want to talk about family? When were you going to tell me your father is an ex-con, huh?"

I rear back in shock, as if Don's hand just darted out and slapped me. In a way, his words are a knockout blow because… "How do you know that?"

He tosses a hand dismissively. "My parents hired a PI."

"Your parents? A PI? Why?"

"Well, now that we learned the truth about you, your family, don't you think it was a smart idea?" he rationalizes.

The truth about you. Your family.

My heart squeezes painfully, a lack of oxygen pumping through my body at Don's insinuation. No one knows the truth. No one except me, Mom, Dad, and maybe, maybe, my stepfather Mitch. But certainly not Don.

And what the hell does that say that I never confided the truth in my fiancé? I swallow back some of my spite because that *realization* stings too. Deep down, did I know that Don wasn't the one? Other examples zip through my mind. Don taking calls late at night, that one time he came home smelling like Chanel Chance even though I'm a Viktor&Rolf Flowerbomb loyalist, the way his mother has been dragging her feet on our wedding menu.

Wouldn't a normal fiancée question him on those issues? Wouldn't a loving, committed fiancée be able to tell him the whole truth of her past? All the sordid details and painful memories?

Don sighs again, as if breaking our engagement is taking too much of his precious time. "Look, you know how my family is. We're a pillar of the community here, of the *country*. I can't—*we* can't afford the type of negative press this type of acquaintance would cause."

"Are you referring to our *marriage* as a mere acquaintance? Who the hell wrote your breakup speech? Your mother?"

Don grips the back of his neck and I roll my eyes.

"Whatever, Don. Fine. You found out my big, bad secret. My father used to be in prison."

"For fraud!" He points at me, as if that proves everything.

"Right," I agree, not expanding on it. "And instead of asking me about it, about anything, you and your family decided that our engagement is finished. Is that it?"

Again, he averts his gaze. He nods. He's a fucking coward. Who lets their parents decide who they marry anyway?

"Okay," I say, standing. "Well, then—"

"They're not firing you or anything. I mean, they're happy to settle, give you a package and a recommendation, but after the Felton-Lawrence wedding okay? They really want you to stay on until after the wedding. Heather Felton requested you personally."

Wow. I'm going to take my shoe off and hit him with it. How did I ever think I could marry Don? Worse, belong to and build a *family* with him?

I squint, as if seeing him for the first time.

Right now, after *this* conversation, I don't see the handsome, charismatic, charming man I fell for. I don't recall the way his eyes glistened when he proposed or how his arms caught me when I leapt into them.

Instead, I see a smarmy, indulgent, spoiled man-child who still looks to his parents to run his life. To make his decisions. To inform him of his choices.

For someone who almost missed out on the ability to make choices, that seems like the ultimate waste. A life poorly, unintentionally lived.

Disgust rolls over my tongue and even though I'm hurt, a

part of me is also relieved. I don't examine that too closely either. Instead, I roll back my shoulders and stare directly at my ex-fiancé.

"You're right; maybe we did rush into this."

Surprise causes his eyes to widen but then he narrows them, hurt. Welcome to the club, buddy.

I clear my throat. "But that won't be necessary. Consider this my notice. I will stay on for one more month, until the wedding. But not for you or your parents. I'm staying for Heather and Preston. Because I like them. Because they have something real and meaningful, which we clearly did not. The day after their wedding, I'll be gone and the pristine reputation of the Servinos and Lely Prive Resort will remain untarnished by any *acquaintance* with Sofia Carpenter."

Don huffs out a breath, as if I'm being dramatic. Meh, maybe I am. But I'm hurt. Disappointed. In him and in myself. In us.

"I'd like to be moved into my own villa for the next month."

He gapes.

"And don't contact me unless it's work related. We are officially finished. Done. I wish you the best. Well, not really, but I'm trying to be civil," I snap.

Don's eyes widen.

"I'm going to pack my stuff now. Send me a message when my villa is ready." I move to leave his parents' private suite, one similar to the space they were gifting us as a wedding present. Well, that's never going to materialize.

"Wait." Don jumps up. "That's it? Aren't you going to, I don't know, cry?"

I arch an eyebrow. "Over you? No, Don. I have survived the lowest of the low. You breaking up with me without even knowing the truth has demonstrated that I dodged a freaking bullet. Yes, I am hurt. Yeah, I'm a little pissed. But I'm not broken." I flash him a bitter smirk and swipe up my purse. "Men like you can't break women like me."

I make my way back down to the suite I share with Don at the most beautiful, enchanting, private resort on Maui. Eight months ago, I moved here to support Don's career when his parents named him the General Manager of the resort. They gave me a job on the event planning team. It's a fast-paced world, being in operations, but as someone who regularly volunteers to plan galas and charity events at the hospital, or the prison, I adapted quickly.

And I loved having the chance to experience the true beauty of Hawaii.

I enjoyed the magical sunsets, the ones that painted the sky vibrant hues of fiery orange and gold. I was mesmerized by the rich aquatic life. I lived a dream life and I still have the opportunity to do so for another month. Sans Don.

I enter the suite and beeline to my closet. I pull down a bunch of clothes, haphazardly stuffing them into a suitcase. I drop my shoes on top. I'm packing up my bikinis when the first wave of sadness sweeps through me. It intensifies tenfold when I spot the white garment bag at the back of my closet.

My wedding dress. It's the first one I tried on and the moment the soft chiffon whooshed against the tops of my feet, *I knew*. This was the dress. I bought it on the spot and have had it hanging in my closet since that day, almost eight months ago. Pulling out the garment bag, I unzip it to gaze at the dress that made me feel beautiful. Whole.

I blow out a sigh. Whole for the wrong man. I zip up the bag and fold it neatly on top of my suitcase. I feel like a fool. On some level, I believed Don was the one. I brought him to Mom and Mitch's retirement party before they left for a cruise around the world. I took him to a handful of my stepbrother Jesse's hockey games in San Antonio. And perhaps most painfully, I told my Dad about him. I welcomed him into my life and really believed he'd stay there, forever, as a permanent fixture.

It's laughable really. I grew too trusting. Hasn't my past taught me anything? Nothing lasts forever. All we get are moments, some last longer than others, and this one just came to a sudden end.

I zip up my suitcase and open my laptop. Pulling up the search engine, I type in the information for a flight to San Antonio the day after the Felton-Lawrence wedding. While I wait for the page to load, I pour myself a shot of vodka and toss it back, letting the burn blaze a path of heat to my stomach. Relief quickly follows when I note a flight for that afternoon.

I book it and pick up my cell phone, relocating to the window. I glance out at the sea, my gaze lingering on the curling waves. The ocean is restorative for me, a place that mirrors my moods. Serene and calm, strong-willed and fierce. It can be either a playground or a tempest but both versions comfort me. It's a kinship I formed a long time ago, when I was a bald little girl seeking treatment at Cedars-Sinai Medical Center in LA. We were there for a handful of months and one day, my dad whisked me away from the beeping monitors and IV lines to Venice Beach. That day, the ocean was playful, spraying us with white foam and receding to leave an expanse of seashell treasures behind. Mom and I collected them while Dad took our photos. That day, I wasn't a sick kid, and my parents weren't separated. We were just a family, and it was perfect. For an entire afternoon, it was perfect.

The following month, my symptoms worsened and Mom and Dad legally divorced but my love for that day, for the ocean, remained. I turn away from the window as pressure blooms in my lower back. I press my palm against it, massaging the skin. Ugh, I'm already having physical manifestations of Don's betrayal.

My phone buzzes and I jump.

DON

Villa 34.

The pressure subsides and I grin. The villa feels like a small victory. Of course, I don't really need a villa, any small room would do. But Don's dismissal of me, his speaking about my father the way he did when he doesn't know anything, *not a goddamn thing*, hurt. My requesting a villa is some petty form of revenge, but now that it's secured, it sure does taste sweet.

In one month, two of America's most prominent families are melding together with the union of Preston Lawrence and Heather Felton.

The resort has hosted many weddings in the eight months I've worked here but this is by far the biggest, the most lavish, and in some ways, the most sincere. While their families are certainly influential and throwing down serious coin on the wedding of the social season, Preston and Heather have been incredibly warm and genuine since I first met them in March when they came to visit the venue. Heather even sent me a bouquet of flowers last week for my birthday.

They're the only reason why I agreed to stay.

I've learned firsthand how cruel, lonely, and empty the world can be. Mostly through my illness but also through Dad's time in prison. On the other side, ironically, both the hospital and the prison offered glimpses of genuine love, sincerity, and commitment. The type that Preston and Heather embody.

I don't care about how this wedding will provide fantastic publicity for the Servino family. It doesn't matter that the Lawrence and Felton names will pull in other high-profile clients. All that matters is that Heather requested me, and I don't want to disappoint her. While Don's dismissal and his parents' disregard stings, Heather's support eases some of my hurt.

Many months ago, we bonded over my volunteer work at the hospital. She even flew in to one of the events in Michigan and, yes, she donated a hefty sum of money, but more than that, she took time chatting and listening to the patients and survivors present. She's one of the shining examples of good I can cling to during this new transition that makes my future feel uncertain.

A prudent woman in my shoes would pray for guidance. Or clarity.

I gather up the rest of my belongings and stack them by the front door.

I've never been prudent. So I'll bank on cold champagne and an ocean view in Villa 34 instead.

CHAPTER 1
THEO

I'm in paradise. The sunshine, the ocean pooling around my legs, the feel of the board beneath my body, it's calming. Relaxing.

It's more than I deserve after the past year but right now, I'm grateful my brother and Heather decided to marry here, in Maui. I know they wanted to have something private, something that wouldn't cause a big media spectacle, which is a relief.

For my career, a hockey player for the NHL team, Boston Hawks, I'm known as Eddie Sims. But here, this week, with my family, I'm back to being Theo, the charming, often aloof, second son of American power couple Lance and Margaret Lawrence. Media attention wouldn't just overshadow Preston's wedding, it would also push me into a spotlight I've shied away from for years. I learned early on that my surname draws attention, the kind of attention that comes with ulterior motives. That's why, professionally I go by Eddie, from my middle name Edward, Sims, from my mother's maiden name. It's partly to protect my parents and their work and partly because of my own ego. I'd like to be judged by my performance on the ice and measured by my own merits, without the help of belonging to a well-known American family.

I catch a wave, effortlessly riding it. When I near the beach, I intentionally fall into the beckoning sea and let it roll over me. It's therapeutic, having a week at this lush resort, spending quality time with Mom and Dad, and celebrating Preston and Heather. While my family doesn't fully understand why I've professionally distanced myself from them, they're still supportive enough to root for me in secret and respect my wishes to not call me out publicly.

Besides, last season I did that spectacularly all on my own. I single-handedly cost my team the play-offs, a shot at the Cup, and that's a regret I have to live with.

"Shit," I swear, dunking my head underwater. Why am I drudging this up now? It's in the past; I can't undo it. All I can do is move forward and try harder, be better this season. Now, I'm starting as the Hawks right wing and I intend to pour everything I am, every energy I have, into getting it right.

Right after I celebrate my brother and Heather's union.

With the sea surrounding me, I gaze back to the string of gorgeous hotel villas my parents rented for the week. Although Heather and Preston's guest list is intimate, our family went all out on their wedding week. I need to get back into a celebratory mood; Preston and Heather deserve it. As best man, I owe it to my brother to step up the way he's always stepped up for me.

I dunk myself under water again, letting my failures from last season wash away so I can get in the right headspace to celebrate tonight's festivities.

When my face breaks the surface, I shake the water from my hair, and turn away from the villas. Instead, my gaze falls upon a breathtaking sight.

A woman. A beautiful woman. Tall, lithe, with tanned skin, and a white bikini with ties begging to be tugged. Her hair is wet, molding to the tops of her shoulders. Her face is open, tilted upward toward the blue, cloudless sky.

Where the hell has she been hiding? I've been here for five days and, as best man, I've mingled with every guest present. I'd remember if I met her.

Something about her captures my attention and I'm unable to look way. It's not because she's smoking hot, which she is. No, it's something else.

I watch her for a long moment, glad she doesn't notice me staring. She drags her fingertips through the water, grinning as the little ripples spread outward. She spins once before dropping back into the sea, letting it catch her the way a crowd surfer dives into an expanse of raised arms. With trust and hope and an edge of recklessness.

When she emerges, she twists her hair, wringing out the water. A figure up on the sand waves a scarf to catch her attention. I note the way her shoulders stiffen. She hesitates before lifting a hand in recognition and a streak of pain, a flicker of agony, blazes over her face. I frown, trying to decipher its cause but she's already swimming away, reaching the shoreline, and walking toward the villas. The sashay of her hips flicks away droplets of water, and I swear, gripping the back of my neck, while I try to place her.

She's sexy as hell. But it's something else that holds my interest, that piques my curiosity. It's the heaviness of her gait, the aloofness etched into her expression. It's her disappointment in being interrupted when she was just trying to enjoy a moment to herself. It's her desire to remain unseen, otherwise she would have swum on the other side of the resort, amid the group of people trying to catch everyone's eye.

She's an anomaly in a paradise filled with beauty, laughter, and excitement. Something about her sadness, her realness, draws me in and I'm unable to look away until she disappears into a villa.

"THANKS FOR DOING THIS, THEO." My brother clasps my shoulder.

"Of course," I reply. For Preston, I'd do pretty much anything. Not only because he's my big brother and I've always looked up to him, but because he backed me hard when I wanted to take Mom's maiden name. It took my parents a minute to come around, but Preston advocated on my behalf, no questions asked, since day one.

"It means a lot to Heather too," he adds.

I glance at my soon-to-be sister-in-law and smile. Heather Felton has been a permanent fixture in my life since I was a freshman in high school. She and Preston fell hard and fast for each other, much to the delight of both of our families. They truly are a match made in heaven and even though it's cliché as hell, it's also a rarity. "It means a lot to be included."

Preston squeezes my shoulder once and drops his hand. Heather walks over to us, and Preston tucks her into his side.

I lift my Negroni in their direction. "Cheers to the happy couple."

"Thanks, Eddie." Heather grins, her face radiant. "I can't wait to marry you," she says to my brother.

"Me too, love." He kisses her nose.

And…that's my cue. I drain my glass and make my way toward the bar. "I'll take another one, please."

The bartender smoothly makes my Negroni, placing it down in front of me on a coaster created from crushed seashells. I can't imagine how much time Heather spent on the decor for this week, but I know for a fact that every tiny detail received her stamp of approval.

I turn, letting my back settle along the edge of the bar. Bringing my drink to my lips, I survey the room. Beautiful dresses created from a multitude of textures and colors, a seriously strong watch game on full display, blinding diamonds, and—wait.

I squint, my gaze zeroing in on the woman. The beautiful woman from the sea, blending in with a floral display that mimics Monet's Garden at Giverny. But how could such elegant, natural beauty ever blend at an event like this?

Pushing off the bar, I make my way toward her. She doesn't notice me coming, which gives me time to study her. Dark hair that's a bit unruly snakes into waves that hang down her back and falls around her shoulders. Tanned skin, with a dash of pink in her cheeks and the tip of her nose from exposure to the sun. Freckles decorate the slope of her nose and the tops of her cheeks. They make me smile because I'd bet my signing bonus that every other woman in this room went to great lengths to cover up their freckles. I like that this woman embraces her natural look. Hell, aside from a swipe of mascara, I don't think she's even wearing makeup.

I'm only a few paces away now and my gaze dips lower. Jesus. Her body is somehow sexier now, encased in a simple, form-fitting black dress, than it was in a white bikini. Spaghetti straps cross her shoulders, giving a full look at her toned, tanned skin. Her dress molds to her curves, slim waist, full hips, long legs, ending just below her knees.

She looks up as I approach and freezes, her mouth dropping into a startled "O." I narrow my eyes, wondering if she gives that expression when experiencing a different kind of O.

Get your head out of the damn gutter.

"What are you doing here?" I ask her. Shit. That's not how I wanted to start this exchange but, "Who are you?"

A hint of panic flares in her eyes but then she closes them. She rolls her shoulders back, stands to her full height, pushing out her impressive chest, and fixes me with a cool stare that fascinates me just as much as her unease from a moment ago. More questions roll through my mind and suddenly, I want to know everything about this woman when I usually don't give a shit if I even learn a girl's name before taking her into my bed.

But that's not what this is about, is it?

"My name is Sofia," she gives by way of explanation.

"Theo." I hold out a hand.

She hesitates for a second before placing her palm against mine. I hang onto her hand a moment longer than necessary, not wanting to let go.

I grin. "Are you having a nice time?"

"Nice enough," she says guardedly.

I bark out a laugh and some of the tension leaves her face. She smiles back and my laughter falters because her smile is so damn…genuine. It hits me full-on, the ease with which it was given.

"I saw you earlier," I admit, not wanting to sound fucking creepy. Is this making me sound creepy? "In the ocean."

"Oh." A sly grin crosses her face. "I saw you this week too. You're a great surfer."

I nod my thanks and gesture to a passing server. I swipe a champagne flute, handing it to her.

She takes it delicately, as if frightened she'll snap the stem of the glass. "Thanks."

"You like champagne?" I never met a woman who didn't but this girl, Sofia, seems unnaturally nervous.

She shrugs, taking a small sip. "I like anything tonight, but I shouldn't be drinking here."

I place a hand in the center of her back, moving us away from the floral monstrosity and out to a high-top table, where the sound of the ocean drowns out the chatter of guests.

"Why's that?" I ask.

She sighs, biting the corner of her lip. She mutters something under her breath, and I lean closer, trying to catch the words. I think she said, "screw it," which makes me smile again.

"This is my last wedding." She wrinkles her nose and takes another sip of her champagne. "I was employed here, and a month ago, I was let go. Well, kind of forced to quit but they asked me to wait until this weekend. Tomorrow's the wedding so..."

Surprise rolls through me. "You work here?"

She tilts her head. "For another twenty hours. I'm pretty much off the clock now but...there was an issue with the flora." She gestures back toward the massive floral wall.

I check it out again. "It looks perfect to me."

"That's a relief," she laughs. "It's fixed now." Her gaze settles on Preston and Heather for a long moment. "They're a beautiful couple. The loveliest, most down-to-earth couple I've met while working here."

I follow her line of vision, watching as Preston twists a strand of Heather's hair around his finger and leans down to kiss her. They're so enamored with each other, they share the same glow, an intrinsic togetherness that not all couples have. "They're the best," I agree. I gave up on trying to create that kind of glow with a woman a long, long time ago. My brother and Heather are the exception to the rule, not the norm. "How do you know them?"

"I helped plan this soiree," she explains, spreading her arm out to encompass the lavish party with so many intrinsic details.

"It's beautiful," I tell her truthfully, impressed by her work. "Especially the flora."

She chuckles, as I intended, and I'm caught off guard by her beauty. I mean, yeah, she's a smoke show, but when she laughs, she's effervescent. Stunning. Elevated in a way that makes her seem ethereal. Like a goddess or a mermaid or something. Listen to me, I'm definitely being fucking creepy. A mermaid?

"I'm sorry about your job. If you pulled this off, then it's their loss. You're seriously talented." I bring my Negroni to my lips.

She blushes slightly, dipping her head. Her shoulders round forward as she shrugs. "Thanks. It is what it is. There's always other jobs, right?"

I roll the Campari over my tongue, considering her words. It's an odd remark because most people either love what they do too much to consider anything else. Like myself. Or Preston. Or they're so locked into their jobs and the lifestyles they provide, that anything else seems scary. Unattainable.

But this girl, Sofia, seems oddly okay with losing her sweet gig at this world-renowned resort. "You didn't like working here?" I press.

She scrunches up her nose. "No bullshit?"

"What?" I sputter, laughing.

"I mean, you want me to be honest?"

"Uh, yeah…" Don't most people want an honest response to a question? I ponder that for a second and realize that, no, most people want the answer they're expecting. I lean closer to this enigma before me, gesturing for her to continue.

"I liked working here. Especially with couples like Preston and Heather, although they're next level. Like, relationship goals."

"Fair."

"You team bride or groom?"

"Both. But I'm the best man."

"Oh, nice." She grins, as if this news excites her. "I see the resemblance now. I can't believe we haven't met sooner. You're Preston's brother."

"Guilty." I grin back. "So, my brother and Heather are your favorite couple?"

"Yes. Most people irritated me."

I bark out another laugh, caught off guard. "Why?"

"Meh. Too pretentious, too caught up in their own head and the tiny worlds they built inside of them to see the beauty a place like this provides. Not the services or amenities but the astounding, natural beauty of Maui."

As she speaks, I glance out to the sea again, watching the waves curl, the foam spray. I look back to Sofia. "You're right."

She lifts her right shoulder an inch before dropping it. "I know."

I smirk, liking her even more. "You are the most refreshingly honest person here."

"Thank you," she says sincerely. "But I don't know if you'll feel that way when you learn the rest."

"The rest of…?"

"My story."

"Oh. Well, do carry on." I drop my elbows to the table, hunching forward. She doesn't back away, but her eyes flare the tiniest bit and the tip of her tongue swipes over her bottom lip. It's clear that I affect her and yet…it's also clear that she's just being herself. That her sharing her story has nothing to do with me and everything to do with her. She'd be just as chatty if she was conversing with Heather. Or Preston. Or Mom and Dad.

Wait. I narrow my eyes for a second, wondering if *that's* what this is about. Maybe I've gotten it all wrong. I've gone by Sims for so long, I've forgotten the appeal of the Lawrence name. Sofia's obviously met Mom and Dad and knows about their expansive network. Maybe she's feeding me the sob story to help her land a new job.

While I've enjoyed this week, taking a break from the public persona of Eddie Sims, I've stepped back into the role of Theo Lawrence, which has its own set of rules. In Maui, I may not be the infamous, wild, partying Hawk who lost the play-offs, but I am known as Lance and Margaret's son, which in many ways, comes with more expectations.

"I do like planning events but not necessarily weddings.

My true calling is volunteering," Sofia says, gearing up for her pitch.

"What kind of volunteering do you do?" I ask cautiously. Here it comes—she wants funding for her next great idea.

"Mostly planning events at the hospital back home in Michigan. Sometimes, the prison too."

Uh, what? My eyebrows furrow as I stare at Sofia, trying to read her expression. Nope, she's serious. She's *really* serious. And surprisingly, not asking for a job or making a pitch, even knowing who I really am. I clear my throat. "The prison?"

"Yeah. I love the tutoring programs to assist inmates with their GEDs or even college degrees. Oh, and the pen-pal programs." She makes a circle with her index finger and thumb, flashing me the "okay" sign along with the cluck of her tongue. "Just things that fill my cup, ya know?"

"Hospitals and prisons," I repeat, wondering if she's messing with me. "What do those two places have in common?"

"People who need support." She says it like I'm being dense.

"Hm," I say slowly, seeing her point. Maybe I am. "And yet, you came all the way to Maui to plan this soiree."

She sighs, sadness washing over her face. "I came for my fiancé."

I jerk back, as if slapped. Glancing around, I look for the dude who must be a second away from telling me to fuck off, but there's no one paying us any attention. Except Heather, who looks even more excited than she did an hour ago. "Your fiancé?"

"Ex-fiancé," she clarifies, and relief fills my veins. After everything that went down last season, I'm done tangling up in drama. I'm done making stupid decisions that have real consequences. Consequences that don't just blow back on me but on my entire team. "We just…well, he called off our wedding a month ago. That's why I quit, or was fired, whatever. His parents own the resort."

I narrow my eyes, realizing that her eyes are clouded over. Shit, she's a little tipsy. From the champagne? Or… "Have you been drinking?"

She hiccups, holding up her hand again. This time, she places her thumb and index finger an inch apart. "Little bit. But shh, don't blow up my spot because…the flora really is something else."

"It is," I say softly, my heart going out to her. A few months ago, I would have blown her off. Eddie Sims from last season didn't have the patience to deal with drunk girls hung up on their exes. But since coming home this summer to spend time with my family and reevaluate my priorities, I've grown more into the Theo Lawrence of my past. The guy who once wore his heart on his sleeve, until it was shattered. But that guy can certainly empathize with Sofia. "I'm sorry about your engagement."

"Thank you."

"But Don Servino seems like a massive douchebag," I tack on. While his parents are all right, he's showy as fuck. I mean, the whole family had dollar signs in their eyes when they met with my family to discuss the wedding, but Don seemed slimy about it. How the fuck did a guy like him land a girl who volunteers at hospitals and prisons? And knows shit about exotic flora?

Sofia laughs and shakes her head. But I catch the tears that pool in the corners of her eyes. "Everyone caught on to that little factoid much earlier than me."

"Hey." I move my hand over the table until it touches her wrist. "I've only known you for thirty minutes and I promise, you're better off without him."

"How can you tell?" she whispers, her expression curious.

"Because any woman who loves volunteering, who cares about the GEDs of inmates, and who can still sincerely celebrate the union of two people mere weeks after losing her own happily ever after is a unicorn. And Don Servino isn't deserving of most women, never mind unicorns." Inwardly, I groan. A fucking unicorn?

Her expression smooths out and she gives me a smile. A real one that makes her face glow similar to Heather's. One that informs me that unicorn was actually the way to go. "Thank you, Theo. It's a little bittersweet, my last wedding. And with my favorite couple. But that's the nicest thing anyone could have said to me tonight. And I'm happy it was you."

"Me too," I reply, caught off guard by her honesty.

"Can I tell you a secret?"

I lift my eyebrows. *There's more?*

"This is my last night here and…"

"And?"

"I want to do something fun. Something wild. Maybe a little reckless. I think I tried too hard to be the woman Don wanted me to be. Clipped my own wings, as pathetic as that is to admit. I used to be so damn spontaneous…"

I shake my head and laugh, squeezing her wrist once before dropping it. "One last hurrah?"

"Something like that. Tomorrow, I fly to my brother's in San Antonio but tonight…" She drifts off again, her gaze on the ocean. "It's too beautiful to waste."

"Much too beautiful," I agree, staring right at her. I've never met anyone like Sofia before. She's…captivating. In a way I'm not sure if I should lean into or back away from. She's blatantly honest and sincere. But she's also hard to get a read on. It's almost as if she could disappear in an instant. Too intangible to hold on to.

"Want to start with a drink?" I ask.

She grins, shaking her empty flute. "I'd love that. I'm all out."

"You and I both know that can be rectified. Come on." We walk back toward the bar. "Pick your poison."

"Are we going all out?" A glimmer of excitement rings her irises.

"What do you think?" I ask, enjoying being with her more than surfing in the sea.

She glances at the bartender. "We'll take two shots of Beluga..." She peers around him to glance at the bottles. "Epicure. Chilled."

The bartender nods and I let out a whistle. At six-thousand dollars a bottle, this chick is going all in. And I fucking love it.

"You don't mess around, Sof," I joke, shortening her name. It's something I haven't done in ages, preferring to keep the girls I tangle up with at arm's length. But something about her sincerity pulls me closer, makes me feel like I've known her for longer than tonight.

She flashes me a grin, but her eyes are serious. "No. Not anymore. I'm all about the moments."

I inch closer, until my arm brushes against hers. "I'm glad I met you."

She smirks, picking up the shot glasses and handing me one. "To being real."

"The realist," I agree, tapping my glass against hers and tossing back the vodka.

It's smooth and cold, but burns a trail all the way to my stomach.

Behind us, aimless chatter and boisterous laughter ring out, mixing with the delicate sounds of a harp. But here, at the bar, it's just me and Sofia and the unmistakable tug of possibility.

She takes her shot without flinching and tosses me a smirk.

I grin back.

A promise and a warning flash from her eyes. Oh, she's trouble.

And tonight, I'm sure as hell going to enjoy it.

CHAPTER 2
SOFIA

"We're really just going to leave?" I question him, glancing around the space. For sure, I've got a solid buzz going on from the vodka shots I tossed back with my new friend, Theo. But as the best man, can he really walk out of the rehearsal dinner?

As a woman supposed to be *working*, I know I *shouldn't*. But since this is my last wedding and the night is going smoothly, it won't take much (read: any) convincing from Theo to have me toeing off my sandals and following him to the beach. I may have lost myself with Don, but now that *that's* over, I know better than to waste moments.

I officially entered complete remission when I was seventeen years old. With no traces of leukemia lingering in my body, my oncologist assured me I had a favorable future ahead of me. Still, I couldn't let the uncertainty of not having a tomorrow go.

My first three years of college, I threw myself into the experience with gusto. I rushed a sorority and took theology and philosophy courses for engaging discussions and the opportunity to view the world through different lenses. I stayed up late with my friends, discussing trivial matters and profound concepts.

And then, I met Don. He signaled to me that it was time to grow up. That there was no room for rash decisions and emotional reactions in his family. So I tempered my spirit and…grew up.

But tonight, my spirit, my mom would say impulsiveness, is surging ahead. Giddiness swims in my stomach and breathless anticipation squeezes my chest. Being here tonight and talking to Theo have resurrected remnants of my past. I used to hang onto the fleetingness of spontaneity, of adventure, with both hands. Tonight, I want that again.

Looking up at Theo, I realize how much I want to reclaim the old me. I don't want to get a good night's sleep, work my way through a mental checklist for tomorrow's wedding, and catch a flight to San Antonio.

I want to enjoy *this* moment with *this* man.

Logically, I know I should *not* be making heart eyes at the best man. But when have I ever considered logic when there's life to be lived?

The corner of Theo's mouth hitches and he winks. Good God, how can I *not* make heart eyes at *him*?

I've watched the sexy surfer ride waves all week long. His hair is longer, and when wet, it's slicked back behind his ears, ending at his collarbone. His eyes are a bluish-green, vivid and open, inviting and tempting. And his body, his body is a piece of art, all muscles, sinewy strength.

I'd be lying if I said I hadn't checked him out this week. All week. Not just because of how undeniably attractive he is, but because he rides waves like the water is an extension of him. Like he's one with the sea, leaning into the rhythm of the waves with perfection. His performance is a hard one to ignore so when I'd spot him walking down his private beach access toward the ocean, I'd stand in the doorway of my villa for an extra moment, appreciating the tourist who seems to love the resort for its unique placement in Maui, and not just for its five-star service.

Now, that tourist is Theo. And the connection I've forged with him over champagne and vodka is even better than watching him surf. It's so instinctive, that I don't want to say good night. I smile back; I'm *not* saying good night.

"Absolutely." Theo threads his fingers through mine and a jolt of electricity zips through me at the touch. So…I am more than buzzed. "Come." He tugs me around the side of the bar, behind the lush floral display I've spent hours perfecting.

When we're adequately hidden from view by the tropical flora, Theo leans forward. So close, I breathe in his cologne. It's like breathing in the beach, a healthy dose of sea air with a wisp of salt.

I wrinkle my nose at Theo. "You sure you want to hang with me? I'm on the Servinos' shit list." That reminder would make most men run for the hills.

But not Theo. No, he laughs. "You think I give a shit about them?"

His dismissal makes me grin. For too long, I fell in line with whatever Don dictated. I thought I was being supportive and understanding; turns out, I was being a damn doormat. The realization angers me, even a month later, because I should know better than to let anyone have a say in my choices. Choices are a luxury and shouldn't be taken for granted.

With that thought in mind, I lean into Theo, enjoying the feel of his arm as it wraps around my shoulders.

Theo walks us closer to the sea and I match his stride, liking the way our shadows look, side by side, on the sand. Soft moonlight and torches leading to the party light up our path, but other than the floating notes of music, we're alone.

I glance up at him. Tonight, I'm reclaiming myself. I'm living in this moment with this man, seizing each second, and feeling the uninhibited deliciousness of being alive. My sandals press into the soft sand and little grains stick to my ankles. The weight of Theo's arm settles more firmly on my shoulders. A light breeze rustles through my hair.

I'm a lucky woman, a benefactor of second chances and do-overs. If Theo promises me tonight, I'm going to take it, enjoy it, revel in it until sunrise.

This moment belongs to me. To us. And I'm good at grasping moments, minutes, with my entire heart and living in the midst of them.

"Sof." Theo's breath tickles the shell of my ear, more seductive than the Maui breeze.

"I've never met anyone like you," I tell him truthfully. "I think you're the most sincere man here."

He freezes, his eyebrows pulling low over his eyes. Fascinating eyes. Blue and green and gold, like the Maui sea at sunset. The corner of his mouth curls upward. "*Here* is filled with prominent members of American society, of French nobility, hell, there's even English aristocracy. Trust me, I'm nothing in comparison. Just a regular guy."

"What do you do?" I ask, suddenly desperate for the answer.

Theo hesitates and a shiver dances down my spine, a warning. But then he clears his throat. "I'm…well, right now, I'm a…teacher," he says finally.

A teacher. I smile. Was he embarrassed to tell me that? I freely admitted that I was fired/quit my job and my ex-fiancé dumped my ass. "I think that's a very noble profession."

He chuckles, the sound pulling at something low in my abdomen. "I like you, Sof."

I grin. I like that he calls me Sof. I like that he wants to play hooky with me. "I like that you're a normal guy, Theo."

He dips his head in acknowledgement and pulls me closer. "Ready to get into some mischief?"

I roll my lips together and scan the dark ocean, the rolling waves, the moonlight. I toe off my sandals and sigh as the sand rises between my toes. Before I can bend to retrieve my shoes, Theo does. They dangle off his fingers as he resumes our walk, holding my shoes like it's no big deal. It's something Don wouldn't even think of doing and the gesture, as small as it, soothes a hurt that has barely dulled into an ache since Don cast me aside.

I glance up at Theo, admiring the clean cut of his jawline, the angular planes of his face. His hair is sandy and messy, like he ran his fingers through it. And I like that too. I'm so over the perfectly coiffed, perfectly dressed, perfectly boring man Don turned into, jumping at every demand his parents gave him. How disappointing he turned out to be. No, I don't want the rules and limitations anymore. I don't want to fit into a mold I'm not supposed to be cast in.

I want the zip and zing, the laughter and truth, the carefree passion of a real connection. No bullshit.

Stopping, I clutch his fingers.

His gaze drops down to mine, but he doesn't say anything, waiting for me.

"Let's go swimming."

Slowly, a smile spreads across his lips. "Now?"

I look up at the beautiful stars, hovering above like twinkling tea lights. The moon is full, round and swollen, like a spotlight. Suddenly, it's as if I'm on stage and the play, my life, my *second chance* at life, is passing me by. If I don't start the performance, if I don't take the lead role, I'm going to miss the whole damn show.

"Right now." I drop his hand.

His eyes hold mine, strong and steady. Real and raw. He unbuttons the long row down the center of his shirt, letting the breeze whip the sides back to reveal washboard abs. My eyes drop on their own accord, and I can't look away.

Wow, he's built. Muscled tendons and ridges I want to drag my finger down. He doesn't call me out on my blatant perusal. Instead, he pops the button on his slacks and lets them drop to the ground. He kicks them off along with his shoes.

I grin, adrenaline and excitement coursing through my limbs.

My eyes snap back to Theo's as he shrugs out of his shirt. I step forward to help, pushing the soft material off his hot skin, my palms slipping over the rounds of his shoulders.

I suck in a sharp inhale and he catches my wrist, holding me close, my body nearly melting into his.

"You sure you want to do this, Sof?" His voice is lower than it was a few minutes ago and a small flicker of relief flares in the pit of my stomach. On some level, I affect him. And thank God, because he more than affects me. He's turned me silent, my tongue too thick to form syllables. "Sofia, babe, look at me."

I do. Whatever he reads in my eyes, in my expression, causes his to soften. He releases my wrist and his hand cups my cheek instead. "We can do whatever you want. No bullshit, remember?"

"I remember," I whisper. "And I want to swim."

"Then let's swim."

I step away from him, now clad in a pair of tight, black boxer briefs. My dress, boring black but fits like a glove, zips up the side. I drag the zipper down, aware that Theo's attention is fastened on me.

My dress drops to the sand and I step out of it, carefully, like stepping out of a puddle. All I have on underneath is a black, lace strapless bra and matching thong.

Slowly, I raise my eyes to Theo's once more.

And the look in his undoes me. Because he's looking at me in a way Don never did. There's heat in his irises, desire causing his pupils to expand. There's pure want in the lines of his face and God, I want it—him—too.

The moonlight casts off his expression, all shadows and

hidden truths, and I hold his stare, memorizing the look he wears.

"Christ, Sofia. You are fucking gorgeous," he nearly growls.

I bite my lower lip, dropping my eyes to the sand. No man has ever spoken to me so honestly before, with so much… sincerity. Not with the scars I bear, etched into my skin as a reminder, clawed into my heart as a warning.

He steps forward, our bare toes touching, and hooks his finger under my chin. His thumb traces the scar on my neck, a leftover from the central line. His eyes narrow and I read the questions in them. Not wanting to ruin the moment, I shift, until the pad of his thumb grazes my collarbone. Theo frowns. "Don't hide from me, beauty. Don't hide from yourself."

His words are an electric current to my heart. Because how does he know? How, in a handful of hours, does this stranger, this man who doesn't really know the inner workings of my life, of my past, *understand* me?

He brushes a kiss over my forehead and my eyes drop as I revel in the feel of his lips on my skin. A coolness replaces the heat of his touch, and he takes my hand again.

Wordlessly, we walk into the sea. The water rises, warm and gentle, kissing our thighs, hiding our hips, swallowing our shoulders. When we're out far enough that the music from the party barely reaches our ears, I float on my back. The stars twinkle above, a scattering of glitter confetti. "I miss this."

Theo chortles. "Crashing rehearsal dinners? I find that hard to believe."

I laugh. "Let me rephrase. I haven't done anything like this, something fun and spontaneous, *with a man*, in a really long time." My feet find the ocean floor and I stare at Theo, waiting for his reaction.

Surprise flashes across his expression. He treads water

closer to me, our knees and arms brushing against each other's. "Don?"

I shake my head. "In the beginning…maybe, there were moments. But the longer we were together, the more I was a pawn in his life. I just didn't see it. Now, I realize he was modeling me into the wife he wanted me to be. But when his parents pointed out a better way, he dropped me real, real fast."

"You feel like he used you?"

I nod slowly. "And the worst part is, I tried to be what he wanted me to be. I tried so fucking hard. Pathetic, isn't it?"

"No." His gaze is severe, intense. "I've done that too. Once for a woman, then for my te-, my friends. For years, I tried to be perfect and in the end, I messed it all up."

"I don't believe you. You are…well, look at you." I gesture at his ridiculous physique, his model-worthy looks. Plus, he's a teacher. Someone who gives back to his community, who shapes the minds of the next generation.

Theo gives me a sad smile. "I'm far from perfect, Sofia. Far from being the good guy."

I narrow my eyes. "I find that hard to believe."

"Well, I find it hard to believe that any man would want a woman other than you." Theo's hands find my hips. He pulls me toward him, until my chest bumps into his. His mouth is so close to mine that I can practically taste the Campari on his tongue. "Stay for the wedding tomorrow."

"I'm working the ceremony. Until my flight."

"No." He shakes his head. "Stay. For all of it. Be my date."

I pull back in surprise. "Your date."

He presses a kiss to the side of my neck. "Yes."

I squirm, his lips so close to my scar. My shoulder lifts toward my ear and Theo pulls back. "But people will…talk," I falter, knowing exactly what the Servinos will say. They'll think I jumped into Theo's bed to spite Don and yet, that would be so far from the truth. I want to jump into Theo's bed because being with him tonight is making me feel more like myself again. And I almost forgot what a gift that is, to be myself.

"Do you care?" he asks, kissing the other side of my neck.

Goosebumps break out along my skin, and I lift my shoulder to my ear again, this time involuntarily. Theo chuckles and kisses my collarbone instead. "Theo," I murmur.

"Sof."

My fingers wrap over the tops of his shoulders, gripping for leverage. He shifts us toward shallower water, until his feet can touch the sea floor. His hands wrap around me, and my legs encircle his hips. I relax in his arms, feeling more comfortable with him than I have with Don for months. "If we only have tonight…"

"This weekend. Say yes, Sof."

I pull back to look at him. A thrill rushes through me. "You really want me to be your date?"

"I really do."

The sincerity in his eyes, the meaning behind his words, invigorates me. In this moment, I feel more alive than I have in years. I don't want to leave the sea, or Theo's arms. I want to stay right here, reveling in this extraordinary moment with this man who seems too good to be true. "Okay."

"Okay," he whispers, smiling back.

"This feels…real. Right?" I can't keep the thread of hope from my tone, and I know he hears it because an almost pained expression streaks across his face.

But then it's gone and he's holding me even closer. "It's real for me too, babe." He lowers his mouth and I lift my face and when our lips touch, I close my eyes and *feel*.

The softness of his lips, the hardness of his jaw, the skillful slip of his tongue as it enters my mouth, pressing against mine. I open up for him slowly, tentatively, but in mere minutes, Theo coaxes out things I've never felt before.

Not truly.

I feel safe in his arms. Wanted and cherished and treasured.

His hands and fingers explore my body languidly, like we have all the time in the world. Like he wants to take his time, enjoying this as much as I am. To him, I'm not a task to cross off a list, but a moment to savor.

A moan comes from the back of my throat and Theo's breathing hitches. I'm molded against him now, his fingers in my hair, his tongue in my mouth.

"I want you, Sofia. Christ, do I want you."

"Then take me, Theo." I toss out the words like a challenge and he pulls back, a glint in his eyes. He holds my gaze for a heartbeat before crushing me against him, his mouth hard on mine.

I revel in every second of it. But instead of losing myself in him, I find myself again.

CHAPTER 3

THEO

S he tastes like sea and sunshine, but her curves are pure sin.

I clutch her, groaning as her slippery skin slides against mine. Her thighs cinch tighter around my waist, and I grab a delicious handful of her sweet ass, deepening our kiss.

What the hell am I doing? I'm sure ditching the rehearsal dinner to sleep with a member of the hotel staff, ahem, former staff, at Preston's wedding is a no-go. It's the kind of drama I'm steering clear of now.

"More," she murmurs and my cock twitches.

But fuck, how the hell am I supposed to turn this—*her*—down?

I pull back, my face tilting toward the sky as she trails a line of kisses down my neck, biting my shoulder. Stars twinkle overhead, the waves a gentle caress against our coupling, and—

"Dammit!" I wince.

Sofia pulls back. "What's wrong?"

"Stepped on a seashell," I admit.

She giggles and it's the greatest fucking sound I've ever heard.

"Come with me," I rasp out. My voice is rough, my control slipping. But I can't fuck this girl in the middle of the ocean. No, if we do this, it needs to happen behind closed doors. I won't have anyone at this wedding speaking poorly of Sofia. And I definitely don't want the resort staff gossiping about her either.

She frowns. "Where?"

I lick my lower lip and she catches the movement, her eyes blown with desire. With want. With every damn thing I'm sure mine are reflecting back.

"Sofia," I falter, not wanting to corner her. Does she truly want this? With me? Would she want it if she knew I'm not a teacher, but a hockey player? That's a hell of a lot less noble than preparing kids for the future, for life. Would she look at me with admiration in her eyes if she knew that during last season's play-offs, I spent the night in lockup, made it so my friend and teammate wasn't there for his pregnant wife, *and* cost the Hawks a shot at the Cup? Would any woman want to tangle up with a selfish prick like that? Absolutely not. "You don't want to do this with me."

Her frown deepens. "Why not?"

"Because," I sigh, untangling her arms from around my neck. "Because I'm not the right Lawrence. I'm the fuckup, the one who—"

She places her finger over my mouth, silencing me. "Does this feel right to you?" She glances down to where her legs still encircle my hips. "Right now?"

I nod.

"Then take me with you, Theo."

I like that she calls me Theo. After hearing women moan Eddie for so long, it feels good, right, to be Theo again. Sure, I was once naive and in love, but I was…less jaded then too.

She flashes me soulful bedroom eyes I want to drown in and I groan. Pulling her with me, I wade out of the sea. I scoop Sofia up into my arms and she laughs, her wet hair tickling my forearm, as I carry her back to my villa and deposit her in the center of my bed.

"We're getting the sheets all wet," she says, jumping up.

"Then get naked." I pull off my wet boxers. For a second, I think about our discarded clothes on the beach but, knowing the discreet nature of the housekeeping staff here, I bet they're cleared away before my family are any wiser.

Sofia grins at me and pops the clasp on her bra, letting it fall away.

"Jesus," I mutter, drinking her in like a starving man. In a way, I am. I haven't done this in a long time. Not the sex part, but the savoring. The appreciation for the fullness of a woman's breasts, for the smooth expanse of thigh and the dip of a waist. Sofia shimmies out of her thong and flings it at me. It hits me in the cheek and we both laugh. "Why does this feel so natural with you?" I murmur aloud.

"Because I'm fun to be with."

"Can't argue that."

"And because you're real." Her eyes are serious when she says it.

A pang of guilt cuts through my chest. Because while I'm certainly being real with Sofia by giving her the version of the man I *want* to be, I'm not telling her the truth. Tonight, she met Theo Lawrence, but as far as the country is concerned, I'm Eddie Sims. I'm the fuckup hockey player with a bad reputation. I'm not deserving of a woman like Sofia.

Her hand settles in the center of my chest and I let out a ragged breath, wanting to erase every thought of Eddie and the mistakes I've made.

My hand wraps around her wrist, anchoring her palm to my chest. "Also true."

"And because after this weekend…" She trails off, lifting an eyebrow.

"We go home."

She nods. "San Antonio for me. And you go back to…"

"Boston," I confirm.

"Boston," she repeats, surprise flashing in her eyes.

"You ever been?" I place my hands on her hips, squeezing.

"Not yet," she murmurs, still a little dazed.

I drop my face to hers, breathing in her exhales. "One day, maybe you can visit?"

She snorts. "I'm all about the moment, Theo. Don't give me false things to look forward to."

At the sound of my name, I stop listening. Instead, I kiss her. I kiss her hard and fast, sweet and slow. I lay her out in the center of my bed and work her over, coaxing her body to peak and crash with mine. I wrap her in my arms, hold her close, and fall asleep with her scent invading my dreams.

The next morning, I order us waffles and hot coffee. I revel in Sofia's laughter and spend extra time wrapped up in her. It's so good, I don't want it to end, which surprises me since I normally avoid morning-afters like STDs. But with Sofia… why does something so fleeting feel like it could be permanent?

"OH, IT'S BEAUTIFUL," Sofia breathes out as we catch our first glimpse of the venue for today's ceremony. When we finally climbed out of bed, she told me she needed to check on everything. While a gentleman would've offered to accompany her just because, I offered to stretch out our time together. Make it last.

The unrivaled beauty of Hawaii wraps around us, and I can't help but agree as I take in the stretch of sea, the cerulean blue sky, the big flowers and deep green fronds. An aisle strewn with petals leads to a rustic arch that probably cost more than a normal person's home down payment. But adorned with flowers, in the center of rows of white chairs, even a non-romantic like me can admit it's breathtaking.

But not as breathtaking as the woman beside me. I take Sofia's hand and lace our fingers together.

She shoots me a crooked grin. "You're making me hopeful, Theo. Don't break the rules."

"What rules? We're being real. Doesn't this, right now, feel right?" I toss last night's words back at her.

She wrinkles her nose and it's cute. "It does. That's part of the problem, isn't it? This feels right but…"

"But we're going home."

"To two different states. With two very different lives, families."

I tip my head toward her. "You never told me about your family. Are they—"

"Theo!" Preston spots me and calls out, waving an arm. His gaze flicks to Sofia and he squints, trying to place her. As soon as he does, he grins. "Morning, Sofia!"

Sofia waves back to him and removes her other hand from my grip. "Best man duties call."

"I guess so," I agree reluctantly. "What are you going to do? Swim? Spa? Whatever you'd like, just charge it to the villa."

She gives me a soft smile. "Don't worry about me. Just, be there for your brother."

"Save me your first dance? At the wedding?"

"Promise," she agrees.

I give her a smile, a real one, and lope off to meet my brother.

"Happy wedding day, man," I tell him.

"Thanks." He grins, looking at the space. "Looks good, huh?"

"Heather's going to love it."

"Hope so." Preston palms my shoulder as we walk toward the restaurant.

"What can I help with? I'm here for whatever you need."

He chuckles. "You think you can redirect my focus that easily?"

I lift my eyebrows. "On your wedding day? Yes."

"Not a chance. Sofia, huh?" He dives right in, his elbow poking me in the ribs.

"Sofia," I murmur. "She's lovely."

"Lovely?" he laughs. "She must have made some impression. You've ignored every pass women, and some men, tossed your way this entire week and on the last day, you take the wedding coordinator up on her offer."

"My offer," I correct. "She's…special."

"Yeah. She did an incredible job, and Heather adores her."

"Heather's got good taste." I gesture toward the venue space. "Today, let's focus on you and your happy future. Tell me what you need."

"Breakfast would be good."

"You got it," I say, ignoring the waffles I consumed less than an hour ago.

Preston and I walk over to the open-concept restaurant, designed around a massive tree trunk, and take a seat. As the waves roll in the background and the breeze skirts through the space, I smile at my brother. "I'm happy for you and Heather. For real."

"I know you are, Theo. And when it finally happens to you, I'll be happy too. You need to start letting people in again, learn how to trust."

I shake my head. "You don't know when to quit, Preston."

"Sofia?" he tries again.

"Not going there, man. It's a weekend thing. She's my plus-one. A happy souvenir from your wedding."

My brother laughs and signals over the server. "See, aren't you glad Heather's final headcount included you bringing a plus-one? She was so sure you were going to show up with a date this week. She'll be thrilled to know you're now bringing Sofia."

I grin, nodding that, as usual, Heather was right. "I only wish I had a whole week with Sofia."

We order breakfast and spend time together, joking and reminiscing, until Dad pulls us away for a friendly game of tennis.

"Friendly, my ass," I joke as Dad winds up to serve. In all fairness, I one-hundred percent get my competitive edge from him.

"We're gonna let you win, Pres. Since you're getting married today," Dad hollers before he whips the ball.

My cousin Harry, playing on Dad's team, rolls his eyes. "We know you're lying, Uncle Lance."

We all laugh, because Dad is. He can't willingly lose at anything. It's probably why he's so successful, owning everything from retail chains to hospitals. But he's also been an incredible role model for Preston and me, stressing the importance of family over everything. Even business. While a lot of the siblings in our social circle compete for their parents' attention, or try to outdo each other for wealth and status, Preston and I have always been each other's biggest supporters. I credit our parents for raising us to be that way.

I twist the handle of my racket. "Don't worry, Pres. We got this."

"We always do, Theo," my brother says.

I dip my chin. Maybe this season really will be my year. Maybe all I needed was to come home, stop being party guy Eddie Sims, and remember who Theo Lawrence is. Maybe all of this—Preston's wedding, Dad's guidance, meeting Sofia— are signs of better things to come.

AFTER A MORNING SPENT with my brother, I make my way back to the villa. A newfound zing of excitement flows through me. I'm looking forward to the wedding and spending more time with Sofia. I wish I had met her my first day here so our time together could be longer.

Of course, we can exchange numbers and follow each other on social media. But what's the point? I'm starting this season as the Hawks right wing. After fucking everything up so badly at the end of last season, I need to be solely focused on my game, my team. I don't have time for a relationship and definitely not a long distance one.

A relationship? I scoff, shaking my head. Where the hell did that idea even come from? I don't do relationships. Not since Delphine shattered my heart. No, I do casual hookups with no promises and no expectations.

I near the villa and a sourness fills my mouth. Why the hell am I so disappointed at the thought of kissing Sofia good-bye, for good, after the wedding? I should enjoy this time I have with her, focus on the now, and have fun.

Opening the door to the villa, I call out, "Sof?"

There's no response. Maybe she did take me up on the offer to hit the spa. The thought makes me smile. I'd love nothing more than for Sofia to enjoy the amenities and services this resort, the one her douchebag of an ex runs, boasts. I bet Don didn't allow her to test out any of the services for herself.

I enter the bedroom and change out of my clothes. Pulling on swim trunks, I decide to get a surf in before Sofia returns. As I'm leaving the room, a purple sheet of paper on the desk catches my attention.

I snatch it up, frowning as I read the words. My eyes dart

to the desk, where a gossip magazine is haphazardly opened to a page. A page of me, with bloodshot eyes and messy hair. It was the night I was arrested, effectively ruining the Hawks chance at the Cup.

Shit, shit, shit. Where did Sofia get this from?

My hand holding the paper trembles as I quickly scan her note.

Eddie,

I had fun last night. Truly. But I can't be your date to the wedding tonight. It's bad enough I slept with you without knowing your real name. Without knowing anything about you, Eddie Sims, NHL player. To pose as your date now when I know the truth is more than my self-respect can handle. Our lie was fun while it lasted, but as I told you last night, I want real.

Have a great season.

Sofia

Fuck. I hang my head back and close my eyes. She thinks I lied about my name, which technically, I didn't. For the first time in years, I was honest about who I am, and the irony of this moment isn't lost on me. But it doesn't matter, my deceit hurt her and hit like a second betrayal.

Anger, at myself, beads in my bloodstream, rushing through me like lightning. Of course, I fucked it up. Don't I always manage to mess up all the things that bring me joy? Don't I deserve this after not being straight up from the jump? Will I ever fucking learn?

I lost Delphine. I almost lost the Hawks. And now, Sofia. Even though we never had a chance, I would have liked to end things on a good note, with some kind of closure. Guilt fills me knowing I hurt a woman as genuine and open as Sofia.

I crumple the paper in my hand and toss it into the trash. I should have known better but, as usual, I didn't realize the severity of my mistake until it's too late. Until I lost the first girl to make me feel in a long time.

That's on me.

Desperate to wash away my sins in the sea, I let the villa door bang closed behind me. Then I grab a board and walk into the ocean, disappointed that this time, there will be no beautiful woman in a white bikini to admire.

CHAPTER 4
SOFIA

"You're serious?" my stepbrother, who is my real brother in every way that matters, asks. His eyebrows are drawn together and he's staring at me like I just announced a move to Mars instead of Boston. "Don't you want to go home? To Michigan? It's probably easier to settle back in there than to start over again."

I flick a hand dismissively. "I need something new. Exciting and invigorating. A fresh start." I don't want to tell my brother just how hard I'll be snubbed in our small town in Michigan. Now that I'm back from Maui, sans engagement ring, everyone and their grandmother has something to say. It's all along the lines of "thought you were too good for here" and "what happened to your ring" and "silly girl, that boy was never going to take care of you." And it's mostly unfolding on social media platforms and in vague conversation threads that don't mention my name. Even though I take it all with a grain of salt, I'd be lying if I said it didn't hurt. It cuts deep. I can't tell if it would be better if they'd just call me out by name. Somehow, being this shadowy "her" is more offensive. "Besides, Mom and Mitch are gone. I'd be on my own there."

Jesse nods in understanding. "They're having so much fun, they may even extend their trip."

I snort. "Our parents are retirement goals."

"For real." He regards me closely. "You sure about this? It's not going to be glamorous. Boston isn't Maui."

"Fuck Maui," I mutter, still hurt over my entire ordeal there. Don, getting fired, *Theo*. Is it alarming that Theo's lie hit me harder than Don's rejection? And now, I'll be moving to Boston, where Theo — ahem, Eddie — lives.

My brother just signed with the Boston Hawks, the same team that Theo/Eddie plays for. When I move to Boston, my path will undoubtedly cross with Theo's. But I don't want to miss out on the opportunity to start over, to go back to college, and to volunteer on a bigger scale. Besides, Boston is closer to Dad.

"I'll be traveling a lot with the team. I'm not sure how much support I can be. But if you're serious about coming, you'll have a place to stay and—"

"I'm serious," I cut him off. "Really, I just need a fresh start."

"Okay," he says slowly, peering at me. "I want you to be happy again."

"I am happy." I sound defensive. Scratch that, I *am* defensive.

He gives me a look.

"I'm *trying* to be happy."

"I know. Don blindsided you and you didn't exactly come home to a support system."

"Mom and Mitch have been great. Their last postcard from Barcelona made me smile."

Jesse reaches across the table and clasps my hand. "All right. But Boston?"

"Boston," I say confidently. "I'm proud of you, Jes. Signing with the Hawks, that's a big fucking deal."

Jesse chuckles. "Let's hope I can live up to their expectations."

"No doubt in my mind."

"I'll be warming the bench."

"You made the team, bro. Work hard and I'm sure you'll be starting in no time."

Jesse shrugs but he's grinning. "Spoken like a true sister."

"I am president of your fan club."

"Yeah." He shakes his head. "If a guy on the team, Sims, wasn't freaking ambidextrous, I'd probably start this season. With Noah Scotch out, the right-wing position was open…"

"Sims?" I ask, hoping I don't sound alarmed.

"Yeah. Dude plays winger, either side, like lightning. He shoots with his left hand just as easily as his right." Jesse shrugs. "But hey, it'll be fun to be roommates again."

I force a shaky smile, the reference to Theo unsettling me. Jeez, I need to get it together or the entire team will know that I slept with the lightning, ambidextrous winger just this summer.

"It's been years," Jesse adds.

"Huh?"

"Since we lived together."

"Oh yeah," I agree. "Not since you left for college." Jesse left Michigan six years ago to play Division one hockey. After graduation, he spent two years in a developmental league in San Antonio. But last spring, things began to change. He signed with an agent, Callie James, and now, he's going to be playing for the NHL Boston Hawks.

"Don't let this shit with Don define you, Sofia. You have a lot to offer; you've just never had a real chance at discovering it."

I nod, realizing that Jesse thinks my reaction is over Don, not Theo. I was enamored with Don. I got caught up in him and his life so quickly that nothing seemed to matter but our future together. Of course, I'd leave school to follow him to Hawaii. Of course, I'd give up my volunteering to plan lavish weddings. I made all the sacrifices and compromises. I made things between Don and me work. That alone should have indicated that I was pretty much in a relationship with myself.

"This will be good for me. I'll go back to college," I announce. "Besides, there's so many wonderful hospitals in Boston; I bet they have even more volunteer programs."

Jesse's mouth hitches into a smile. "And the prison?"

I grin. "Of course, I'll find something to help with there. Plus, I'm closer to my dad."

"Ted won't leave New Hampshire, will he?"

I shake my head. My dad's a mechanic now and has created a small, quiet life for himself after being released from prison six years ago. "He doesn't like to draw attention to himself."

Jesse gives me a sympathetic look and nods in understanding.

"Ugh," I groan. "I can't believe how much time I wasted, Jes. Time, the most precious gift I could ever have. And I wasted it doing things that weren't my passion, to be with a man who didn't truly love me." It's embarrassing how much I made Don's life the center of my world. I orbited around him when I should be orbiting around the things I care about most: people. Volunteering. Providing help and support.

"Why'd you stay with him so long, Sofia?"

I bite the corner of my mouth. I've asked myself that question several times and the answer I keep coming up with is even more pathetic. I heave out a breath. "At first, it all seemed so romantic. A whirlwind I was caught up in. And then, an adventure. Move to Maui, plan beautiful weddings on the beach, and then plan my own gorgeous wedding in paradise. It just seemed like a...fairy tale." I wrinkle my nose.

I know better than to *believe* in fairy tales and yet, when the opportunity presented itself, I couldn't turn it down. "I wanted that great big, all-consuming love and even when I realized that wasn't Don, I didn't fully admit it to myself. I doubled down instead."

Jesse shakes his head. "Tried to will it into existence?"

"Something like that," I agree.

"That's not like you," my brother remarks. He's right. I usually cut my losses but—

"I was trying to be an adult," I counter.

He bursts out laughing and shakes his head. "By staying in a shitty relationship?"

"By being responsible. By proving that there was a real reason for dropping out of college—"

Jesse groans.

"And moving to Maui. For a guy," I conclude.

Jesse gives me a sympathetic look. "Well, now you've got a fresh start to look forward to."

I grin at my brother. "Exactly. I won't make the same mistakes again." As I say the words, an image of Theo filters through my mind.

Jesse lifts an eyebrow.

"You know, the adulting," I clarify. "It's not for me."

Jesse barks out a laugh. "So it's back to being my spontaneous, wild, pain-in-the-ass sister who makes me worry like crazy?"

"Exactly." I grin while Jesse shakes his head.

My thoughts travel back to Hawaii, to that final night. Theo. That night was dictated by the moment, and I lost myself in it. It was fun and heady and next-level sexy. Is that why I was so disappointed to discover Theo lied about his name? Because the moment between us felt so big?

But he also gave me a beautiful night under the stars. Shouldn't I focus on that? On the night we shared? On Theo's quick tongue and hot hands. On the feel of him between my legs and the strength of his back beneath my palms.

I drop my head, feeling myself blush. Not with desire... but with hurt pride. Is that why Theo's lie landed the way it did? It felt like a second slap to the face, when I was still recovering from the shock of Don's. Oh, how furious I was when I saw the magazine, with his name in bold print: Eddie Sims. I hated that the hotel staff must have been talking about me, most likely laughing or muttering about what horrible judgment I have.

The old Sofia, the one before Don, would have laughed it off without a care in the world. In fact, I may even have been impressed by his deceit, his ability to make me believe the lie he wove. But now, since Don and my doubling down, I just feel hurt and humiliated. Theo's deceit feels personal, even though I hardly know him.

Can I be the old me again? The one who laughs off bad dates and easily moves onto the next guy, the next big moment? In college, she was fun and spontaneous, filled with a zest for life. But something about Don and then Theo, something about summer in Hawaii, leaves a sour taste in my mouth. And no matter how hard I try to cleanse my palate, it lingers.

Is this my new norm? Or am I not trying hard enough?

"I'M WORRIED ABOUT YOU," Jesse says as we begin our descent into Logan International Airport.

"I'm with you. I'm fine."

Jesse sighs. "Sofia, you haven't been yourself."

"Jes, my fiancé broke up with me and I just found out, he

gave the same ring to his new fiancée, a different ex-girlfriend."

My brother swears, anger on my behalf rushing over his expression. But after a moment, it clears, and he shakes his head. "Don's a piece of trash. But you know that. Nope, this is something else. I know you're hurt about the way things ended with Don but…is there anything else you'd like to talk about?"

"Nope." I offer a smile. He's right. Learning of Don's newest proposal was certainly a sting, mostly to my ego, but it didn't take me out the same way Theo's lie did. Is that because I felt something real with Theo? Or is it because my ego can only handle so much rejection at once? Whatever the reason, there's no way in hell I can tell Jesse that I'm rattled about seeing his new teammate, Eddie Sims. That I fucked him in Maui and thought his name was Theo. That I believed him to be a teacher. That I accepted his invite to be his date to the wedding of the social season and ditched instead. *Not a chance in hell.*

"I'm really fine," I say easily. But I don't feel easy inside. No, I feel like a brewing hurricane. Hurt, confusion, anger—they all war together for space in my mind. "Really," I reiterate. "Even my dad thinks this move to Boston is a good one. Of course, he's happy I'll be closer, but he also thinks it's a good change of scenery."

Jesse studies me a long moment before nodding. "I'm glad you came with me, Sofia," he says finally, patting my arm.

"Me too."

"And you're sure this is what you want?"

"I'm positive. I want…to really live, Jesse. To be passionate and present and alive, unapologetically alive, in each moment. I want a chance to live my passions. You have hockey. Don't I deserve…something?"

His expression softens. "Of course, you do. I'll support you any way I can."

"Thank you," I say sincerely.

In the next breath, the plane's wheels touch down. As we come to a stop, the flight attendant's voice sounds from the speakers.

"Welcome to Logan International Airport. The current time is 3:42 p.m., and the weather is a balmy seventy-four degrees, sunny and clear skies." She continues her welcome speech and I grin at my brother.

"Let's do this, Jes." I hold out my fist and he bumps it.

As soon as Jesse and I exit business class, we're greeted by an airline representative who whisks us down a corridor, and leaves us with a beaming Callie James, Jesse's agent, in baggage claim.

"Welcome to Boston, Jesse. Sofia." She kisses our cheeks in greeting.

I smile at her. "Hi, Callie."

Jesse pulls our luggage off the baggage belt.

"We've got an apartment set up for you guys. Let's get you home, settled, and then I can run through some things with you, Jesse. If you're up to it, some of the guys are free to grab dinner tonight. One of the players, Eddie Sims, will be your point of contact if you need anything team-specific that I can't provide."

My throat suddenly expands, and I bark out a fit of coughs. Tears well in my eyes as I choke into the crook of my elbow. Callie gives me a concerned look as my brother slaps me on the back.

"You okay, Sofia?" he asks, bewildered.

As my coughing subsides, I nod. "Yeah, sorry. Must have swallowed a bug or something." I give a little smile as Jesse shakes his head at me.

Get it together, Sofia. Who cares if you're going to see Theo? He doesn't mean anything to you. He was one night. A hot moment, a fun memory from Maui. Can't you just leave it at that?

"The team is great, Jesse. I'm here for whatever you need, and you can always reach out to Eddie. Trust me, you and your sister are in capable hands," she says, turning toward my brother as a message alert rings on her phone.

My smile slips. Because as hurt as I am over Theo Lawrence, I can't deny that he does have capable hands. Too capable.

CHAPTER 5
THEO

"No problem," I say easily to my team captain, Austin Merrick. "When's he land?"

"He's flying in today," Austin says. "I'll text you his address."

"Jesse Carpenter," I say the name of our newest teammate. It's standard procedure for new signees to have a go-to guy on the team, and I just became Jesse's. "He's got a wife? Kids?" I ask, wondering what my welcome should include? Do I bring Hawks swag and cupcakes for a cute toddler? Or a bottle of tequila for a bachelor?

"He's single but I think his sister is coming with him," Austin explains.

"His sister?" While it's none of my business, and I clearly don't know the specifics, it's not the norm for anyone to want to uproot their life and relocate to a new city. But maybe Jesse and his sister are super tight? I tilt my head, considering. If Preston was a professional athlete and I didn't have anything rooting me in one place, I'd probably move to be closer to him too. "How old is she?" I wonder. Do I bring her swag and cupcakes?

Panda laughs and shoots me a look. Before I can decipher

its meaning, Cap clarifies. "Don't fuck with Carpenter's sister, Eddie."

I rear back, startled. I'm not planning on screwing with the girl; I wanted to know what the hell I should bring to welcome them to Boston. But now that I replay the current conversation in my mind, I can see where Cap is going. I huff out a laugh and shake my head.

Austin continues. "Last season, you landed your ass in jail during the play-offs. You really want to start this season by flirting with the new guy's kid sister?" The bite in his tone, coupled with the reminder of last season, cuts my chuckle off.

Humiliation and disgust roll through me instead. Last season, I acted like a jackass, an out-of-control social liability, that not only hurt my reputation, but my buddy Yaeger's, and the rest of the team. Then, when I got put in the game, hungover as fuck, I screwed it all up, costing us a chance at the Cup. Last season ended on a particularly sour note, and I swore to myself that I'd start this season off right. No more partying and drinking my face off. No more jail stints and negative attitude. No, this season, I'm putting the team first.

And I just gave my captain the impression that that includes screwing a new player's sister. Shit.

"Not what I meant, Cap," I clarify. "I was wondering if she's a kid sister, like bring her a jersey and a teddy bear, or an adult and grab some Hawks mugs and coffee from The Grind instead," I explain, mentioning my favorite coffee shop in the process.

Panda coughs off his laughter, but Austin's expression clears.

"Oh," he comments, nodding. "Well, good. As far as I know, she's an adult. Coffee's a good call, better than booze."

"I got it covered," I stress. After the way things went down last season, I'm eager to prove that I can step up and do whatever the hell the team needs. If that's a welcoming committee, then I'm going to make sure Jesse and his sister feel right at home in Boston.

"Team's counting on you to step up this season, Sims," Cap continues, stressing *his* point. "Scotch is out, at least until December. And you're the only guy who can take his place, who can play both sides of the ice. That means you're starting as a winger now. If you can't handle—"

"I got it," I cut him off, saying it with more force. Shit, I don't need reminders of last season. Of how Noah Scotch went down, tearing his ACL. He's in rehab after a knee surgery but there were complications and his return to the ice is still questionable. In his absence, the team called me up. Me. And I shit the goddamn bed. But I won't make that mistake again. Not this season.

I clear my throat. "Really, I'm good. Thanks for tapping me."

"All right, get out of here, Eddie." Cap smacks me on the shoulder and leaves the locker room with Panda.

I shut my locker door and sink to the bench. This is my season, my year. If I can play well, keep my nose clean, help propel the team toward a Cup win, maybe I can finally forgive myself for last season. Maybe I can even grow into the type of player, the kind of man, I wanted to become when I first signed with the Hawks.

I shake my head and push off the bench. I take a quick shower to rinse off from practice. Then, I call in an order for the best lobster rolls, pick up a six pack, swing by The Grind, and head to greet Jesse Carpenter and his sister. We'll start this season off right, as teammates, as friends. Hell, maybe even his sister and I will become friends.

YEAH, that's not going to fucking happen.

Because when I knock on the door to Jesse's apartment, which Austin forwarded to me an hour ago, he doesn't answer.

Instead, the woman I haven't stopped thinking about since the first moment I saw her pulls open the door. Sofia's eyes spark with fire when they meet mine, but not the good kind. This inferno is rooted in anger, in hurt, and I feel it burn through my insides, incinerating.

"Sofia," I stutter. She's Carpenter's fucking *sister*? *Real fucking smooth, Sims.*

"*Eddie*," she responds tartly.

Shit. And…*shit*. Because my name, the one I'm known for in Boston, the one girls have been calling me for years, sounds all wrong falling from her lips. Suddenly, I want her to whisper Theo again, in that breathless, needy tone that made me feel like a deity instead of a fuckup.

"What are you doing here?" I blurt out, even though it's obvious.

She smirks. "I'm Boston's newest resident." She holds open the door and I step through, glancing around, bewildered.

I turn toward her, my mind racing. At the expectant look on her face, I swear. "I can explain. I—"

"Don't bother." She blows me off and tips her chin toward a closed bedroom. "Jesse's just in the shower but he'll be out in a minute."

I grip the back of my neck. "Listen, Sofia, maybe I should have introduced myself to you as Eddie. But that week, with my family, I wasn't Eddie. I *was* Theo. I thought you would think it was weird, or that I was fucking with you, when you heard everyone refer to me as Theo. Because my entire family except Heather calls me Theo."

Her eyes are all heat, but the line of her mouth softens slightly, so I keep going.

"My name is Theodore Edward Lawrence," I say, admitting my full name for the first time in years. "My mother's maiden name is Sims. Professionally, I go by Eddie Sims and always have. You've met my family; you know who they are."

Her gaze narrows and I talk faster, half to her, half to myself.

"Instead, you think I'm fucking with you—"

"Fucked." She corrects me. "I think you fucked with me."

I dip my head in acquiescence, even though I hate that she's now placing our entire relationship in the past. As if this, now, doesn't hold any weight. But does it? If she wasn't Carpenter's sister, would our paths ever have crossed again?

I clear my throat. "I wasn't trying to deceive you. The team doesn't even know who my family is. I've always kept my professional life separate from my personal one. I've always wanted to prove I was worth my salt on the ice, and not base it on my surname."

She tilts her head, tapping her chin like she's in thought. And then, sarcastically, "How was the start of the school year? Since you're a *teacher*."

I close my eyes, hating myself for not telling her the truth when I met her. "Look, when we met, I was teaching, coaching, summer camps. I was working with kids. And I loved it."

"So you offered me a fake version of yourself?"

"I gave you the me I wish I was when I met you," I shoot back. My honesty surprises us both.

I pinch the bridge of my nose and take a deep inhale. "Look, I've gone by Eddie for a long time. I never wanted anyone to think I got my position because my family arranged it."

"Arranged it?"

"Through donations, lending money, connections…"

Awareness floods her features. "Oh."

"Or, even worse, that people would try to go through me

to access those connections. To use my family." I chuckle bitterly. "It's happened before and after the last time…it felt safer to use my middle name and Mom's maiden name professionally. Publicly. But when I was with you, I was Theo. I gave you the real me because I liked you. And I wanted you to like me."

"By lying?" she challenges.

"By being the version of myself I want to be. A normal guy, a teacher, who likes to catch waves and take vodka shots with a pretty girl under the stars."

She stares at me for a long moment, but I can't read her expression. It remains flat even as her eyes blaze. "You made me feel stupid," she says softly.

"I never meant to. And I'm sorry."

She shrugs. "Doesn't matter now."

"Yes, it does."

"Why? Because we're going to be seeing each other? Because I'm Jesse's sister?"

"No. Because I still like you."

She rears back, my words catching her off guard. But I mean them.

She releases a shaky breath and I stand still, waiting for her to decide how this is going to play out. Will we be friends? More than friends? Or nothing at all.

The door to the bedroom opens and Jesse, dressed in jeans and a T-shirt, his hair still damp from the shower, comes out. His eyes narrow when he sees me and his gaze swings from me to his sister and back again.

I step forward and hold out a hand. "Hey, Jesse, I'm Eddie. I just wanted to swing by, say welcome to the team. I thought we could hang for a bit. I brought lobster rolls, beer. If you're hungry…" I trail off. I glance at Sofia and place the bag from The Grind in her hands. She takes it warily. "This is for you. Best coffee in Boston."

Jesse gives his sister a look and she manages a small smile.

Her eyes are cloudy when they sweep over me. I've confused her and instead of responding, she backs down.

Her phone rings and relief floods her expression. "It's my dad. I'll be in my room," she says, beelining for her bedroom.

Jesse watches as Sofia closes the door. He shakes his head and turns his attention back to me.

"Thanks for stopping by." Jesse shakes my hand. "Sorry about my sister; she's got a lot going on. I'd love a beer."

"Cool," I say, pulling two from the six pack and tossing him one. What does Sofia have going on? I want to ask. Has she been all right? She looks like she lost weight since I've last seen her. Is she eating enough? Sleeping okay? The thoughts ping through my head but I can't voice any of them because…then I'd have to voice the rest. I clear my throat. "How was your flight?"

He chuckles and sits down on the couch, propping his feet up on the coffee table. "Look, I appreciate your swinging by and bringing food. But I don't want you to feel obligated because the team—"

"It's not like that," I say quickly.

He lifts his eyebrows.

I snort and sit down on the chair opposite him. "I mean, technically it is. But I don't want it to be. You're new to the team and I remember exactly what that was like. I'd like for us to be friends."

Jesse stares at me for a long moment before grinning. "Cool. Me too. Thanks, Sims."

I nod and take a swig of my beer. Shooting a glance to the closed bedroom door, images of Sofia, of that night, flash through my mind, but I shut them down. This season, I'm putting the team first. And the team does not need new, complicated, messy relationships with teammates' sisters.

I lift my beer in his direction. "Welcome to the Hawks."

"Thanks, man. It's good to be here."

We drink to the season and it's easy. As Jesse and I talk

about our families, hockey, and Boston, I realize how much I like him. I think he's a great addition to the team and I genuinely hope we can be friends. We eat lobster rolls, polish off our second beers, and discuss video games. I promise him I'll bring over my Xbox One.

Sofia stays in her room the entire time, but I don't take it personally. Instead, I decide to give her time. Space. And maybe that's what's best for both of us.

Because if I'm going to put the team first, then I shouldn't be thinking of her dark, bedroom eyes or the beauty mark on her left inner thigh. I shouldn't be recalling the sounds she makes when she's close to coming or the line of her neck when her head is tossed back.

And fuck yeah, it's hard. But I do it. I shut it down. Sofia was a vacation hookup. She has no problem seeing it that way, so why the hell is it hard for me to wrap my head around?

CHAPTER 6
SOFIA

"Anything you want to tell me?" Jesse pops his head into my bedroom.

"Nope." I make a popping sound on the "p," not bothering to lift my head from the magazine I'm pretending to read.

I'm still on an article pertaining to the #FreeBritney movement and haven't digested a single word, which sucks, because Britney Spears deserves all our support.

"Seriously?" my brother presses.

I snap the magazine closed and look up, arching an eyebrow.

Jesse grins. "What's the deal with you and Eddie?"

"Nothing. Just met him."

"You seemed annoyed by him."

"He seems like an annoying guy," I shoot back.

My brother snorts and collapses beside me on my bed. He studies me for a long moment.

I huff. "Now you're annoying me."

"How? I haven't done anything."

I toss down the magazine. "Quit staring at me."

"I'm trying to get a read on you."

"There's nothing to read." I cross my arms over my chest, giving every defensive signal in the book.

Jesse rolls his eyes. "You're usually a lot nicer to my friends or guys on my team." He narrows his eyes. "What's going on with you?"

I sigh, taking note of the stress in Jesse's expression. The last thing I want to do is cause him to worry when he's trying to get in with his team, when he's finally made it to the NHL. Three years ago, everyone speculated he'd be a top draft pick but then his mother fell ill, and he dropped everything to be with her. I know he doesn't regret it, especially since those last months with his mom were some of their best, but he has worked hard to get where he is. And that deserves to be celebrated sans my bitchy attitude.

"Nothing." I shake my head. "Just an off day. I'm sorry. I'll be nicer next time."

"I'd appreciate that. Eddie's been assigned my team buddy, which is always fucking lame, but he's actually a cool dude and I think we could be friends so…"

"So…I got it," I say, not adding that I can't be friends with Theo. Because that ship has fucking sailed.

"You settling in okay?" Jesse asks. Again, that note of concern rings in his tone.

I smile, dipping my head. "Yes. I already signed up for some volunteering."

He arches an eyebrow. "Where?"

"Mass General to start…" I trail off.

"And the prison?"

"I start tutoring next week," I admit.

Jesse groans. "Sofia, you know I'm supportive of your volunteering. But do you have to go to the prison? Can't you find a pen pal or something?"

I snicker. "I do that too. He's at the penitentiary in Alabama."

My brother is not amused. "I worry about you going alone. That you'll—"

"Get kidnapped? You know a lot of the guys in the GED program—"

"Are serving life sentences."

"Need a lifeline. Something to give them hope," I counter.

He sighs. "Just, please, be careful."

"Always," I promise. When Jesse looks at me for an extra second, I grin. He's not wrong to worry. In my past, I got myself into a handful of mix-ups, although never due to my volunteering at the prison. My trouble was more of the innocent variety—staying out too late, dating the wrong kind of guys, being so present in the moment that I didn't consider the consequences for my future. Kind of like packing my bags to follow a boy to Maui.

"And tell me what you get into so I can back you up with our parents."

"Duh," I laugh. Not that Mom and Mitch aren't supportive of me, but like Jesse, they worry. Jesse advocated on my behalf when I dropped out of college to move to Maui. Not that he thought it was my best decision, but he still stood up for me with our parents. For him, I'll try harder. I'll be civil, maybe even friendly, towards Theo.

"You know, some of the guys on the team are getting together for dinner tonight. It's super casual. Wives and girlfriends are coming so..." Jesse trails off.

"I'm so in." While I may be the lamest sister on the planet for coasting on the wave Jesse is riding, I'm not going to miss out on a chance to mingle with a girl group and learn about the scene here in Boston.

"I figured. Could be good for you to meet some girls in Boston."

Hell yeah. I haven't had a true girlfriend in a long time. When I left college to follow Don to Hawaii, I lost touch with most of my girl group, my sorority. Now, they graduated and are starting exciting careers. Our lives have gone in different directions. It's my own fault for making Don my world. I won't make that mistake again. "What time are we leaving?"

"An hour." Jesse rolls off my bed.

"Sounds good." I stand too and open my closet door to find an impression-worthy outfit.

Tonight, I start my new life in Boston with no boyfriend to hold me back.

COLORFUL. That's the word that springs to mind when I enter the restaurant. It's Mexican fusion, which is an interesting combination, but the atmosphere is warm and inviting. Jesse spots his teammates and their significant others at a table in the back.

"Hey, man," one of the guys at the table stands. He extends his hand. "I'm Panda. Good to meet you. This is my girl, Abbi."

A friendly brunette waves.

"Nice to meet you," a different girl, with light brown hair and green eyes, holds a hand out to me. "I'm Chloe. Austin is my boyfriend."

Austin, the team captain.

I smile back. "I'm Sofia, Jesse's sister."

"Welcome to Boston. I'm Claire." A blonde grins, her blue eyes sparkling. "I'm with this one." She pokes the guy beside her who turns my way.

"What's up? Easton," he introduces himself.

"Sofia," I say, as Theo pulls out a chair for me. I sit.

Jesse takes the seat beside mine and now, I'm sandwiched in between my brother and the man who once gave me three orgasms in one night. While the entire table is filled with good-looking men, they're all coupled up. The only available option for tonight happens to be the man I can't get out of my head. Damn.

"Hey, I'm Shell. I'm taking care of you all tonight. To the newbies, drinks?" The server appears. She's bubbly and chatty and right now, the person I'm most happy to see.

"Just a beer," Jesse orders.

I glance around the table, cataloguing everyone's beverages. I'm not really a beer drinker but I want to fit in, for Jesse, and for myself.

"The margaritas are great," Claire offers.

"Sold." I smile at Shell.

As she leaves to grab our drinks, the conversation at our table picks up.

"The sushi fajitas are really good," Theo remarks beside me.

I ignore him, intently studying my menu.

After a beat, he chuckles. "Playing it like that, huh?"

I glare.

His smirk widens. "Got your attention."

I roll my eyes. "What do you want, *Eddie*?"

"I wish you'd call me Theo again," he says it simply. He says it in a way that affects me, which irks me, because I don't want to be affected by Theodore Lawrence.

I don't want to be affected by any man anymore unless it's my toes curling, fingers gripping the sheets, head thrown back, and eyes squeezed tight.

Which, I know from firsthand experience, Theo is good for.

"I really am sorry," he says.

I stare right at him, noting the sincerity in his eyes. That's the second time he's apologized to me. Don's never so much as admitted his wrongdoings so even Theo's apology affects me. I feel myself soften toward him, melt into his space, like butter left out to spoil.

The reminder snaps me out of my momentary delusions. That's all I ever am to men, something pretty to be spoiled, tarnished, lied to. A fun night, an exciting moment, a beautiful second in time. Partially, it's my own fault since that's the reputation I cultivated in college. But do I still want that now?

I nod once and shift my menu. "Thanks for the apology, Sims. But I'm not interested."

"At all?" He narrows his gaze, calling me out.

Under his attention, I shift, my thighs pressing together because damn him, I'm lying through my teeth. It's not only my body that wants to inch closer to his, it's my mind too. I want to know what he's going to say next, how he's going to play this. Ugh, what is wrong with me?

Actually, what is wrong with him? Why is he pushing this? Why does he care so damn much? If I didn't follow Jesse to Boston, our paths never would have crossed again. I don't understand his angle and that frustrates me too.

Damn you, Theo Lawrence. I turn my attention back to my menu, trying to block Theo out of my line of sight. It's freaking futile. How can I not notice his hair falling over his forehead? Or the way his pinky finger rests just millimeters away from my hand on the top of the table. How can I shut out the rumble of his voice or the way his laughter rolls through my belly like a curling ocean wave?

"How do you like Boston, Sofia?"

I glance up, relieved that the woman sitting across from me tossed a question my way. Chloe, that's her name.

"I'm not sure yet. We just arrived today. But it's nice to be in a new place. In a big city."

"Where were you before this?" she asks.

"Um, Maui."

Her eyebrows snap together, and I realize I must sound ridiculous. Most people dream of a vacation to Hawaii. It's a luxury "it" place. A true paradise. "Sometimes, we all need a break," she agrees, and I could hug her for not making me feel more awkward than I already do.

"Exactly." I snap my menu closed.

"If you need help with anything as you settle in, feel free to ask. Between the team, and all the girls, we can point you in the right direction."

"Thanks!"

Chloe waves a hand. "Anytime. A few of the girls started over here, in Boston. It's not easy."

"I'm thinking about…going back to college," I offer up. On either side of me, the guys take note. Jesse, because he's too protective to not witness how I'm getting along with the girls. And Theo, because he's fucking nosy.

"Oh, that's awesome!" Claire says. "My cousin Indy, Noah Scotch's baby mama, is a professor at Brighton. You could definitely pick her brain about admissions."

Easton sighs. "His fiancée. She's his fiancée."

Claire waggles her eyebrows. "But baby mama has such a salacious edge, doesn't it?"

Chloe and I laugh.

"Thanks, I'd love to connect with her. I'm also looking into volunteering," I share.

"Cool! Abbi—" Chloe points to the brunette sitting beside the goalie, Luca Pandatelli, as he throws a nacho at the team captain—"runs a bunch of youth outreach events and camps. And Vivi, Yaeger's wife, works with a woman's shelter, Maybelle's House, in the city. You should talk to either of them."

"That'd be great," I say.

"Sofia just signed up for some volunteer events at Mass General," Jesse adds.

"Hospitals and prisons," Theo mutters next to me.

I step down on his foot, reminding him to be quiet. He lifts the toe into the arch of my foot instead. I move my shoe away and note his smirk in my peripheral vision.

"Ooh, do you know which ones?" Chloe asks.

"Vivi's got some kind of collaboration going on between Maybelle's House and Mass General," Claire tosses out.

"I remember reading about Maybelle's House." I squint, as if that will help me recall more about the event.

"Either way, you need to meet Vivi." Chloe smiles.

"Absolutely. Thanks, guys." A burst of excitement rolls through me. I can't believe how easily I'm hitting it off with these women. I don't know what I expected them to be like, but I love that our interests overlap. I was tight with my sorority and made a few surface-level friendships in Maui, but I've never connected with women as passionate about volunteering outside of the actual events before. I brighten immediately at the prospect of becoming more involved in something new, something that creates change and selflessly offers support to vulnerable members of society. I glance around the table, but all the guys are busy in conversation.

"Have you started a degree program?" Claire asks.

I nod. "I was three years in for nursing but…I never finished my degree and…" I trail off. How do I explain that I dropped out of college to follow fucking Don without these smart, successful women not judging me? I don't want to ruin their impression of me this early in our meeting each other. They'll think I'm silly and naive, the way most people must when they hear that I quit my life to move to Maui.

But not Theo. No, that night, he gave me genuine compassion. That night, I was just…me.

I sneak a glance at him to find him staring directly at me. His eyes flash, the same curiosity and intrigue from the night we met, flaring.

"She was dating a loser," Jesse supplies helpfully. "Not dating, engaged, but now that's done and Sofia's getting back on her feet."

"Oh, no." Chloe wrinkles her nose. "I'm sorry things didn't work out."

"Don't be," Jesse and Theo say at the same time.

The table freezes, a strange silence hovering over it.

Jesse narrows his gaze at Theo.

"Damn, Eddie, offering your two cents already?" Panda laughs.

Theo shrugs. "Just saying, if Sofia left school and her volunteering behind, it must have been the wrong guy, right?"

His eyes find mine again, unwavering.

I clear my throat. "I'm here for a…a do-over."

"Good!" Claire exclaims, smoothing over the awkwardness. "Then, let's get together and see what we can do. Want to have lunch this week? Or drinks?"

"Easy, Claire," Easton cautions.

"I'm in," Chloe agrees.

Claire grins at me, her eyes open and trusting, her smile genuine. Feeling like I may have made a friend, all by myself, for the first time since before I got caught up in Don, I smile back.

"Sure."

CHAPTER 7
THEO

"What's the deal with you and Jesse's sister?" my team captain, Austin, asks me.

I place the bar I'm bench-pressing onto the rack and sit up, grabbing a towel off the floor. "What do you mean?"

Panda, our goalie, bursts into laughter. "You're playing, right? Girl was giving you dagger eyes, which means, you hit it and quit it. Or rejected her from the jump. Cap's asking, which is it?"

I quirk an eyebrow, even as my frustration rises. Did everyone at the dinner pick up on the icy vibes between Sofia and me? And why the hell are they calling me out? I was perfectly polite to Sofia. She shut me down, not the other way around.

"We have...history," I say slowly, not willing to kiss and tell. Especially since I want Sofia to give me the time of day again. If only as a socially agreeable woman so things aren't awkward between Jesse and me. I can't have any friction on the team this year, not when I caused so much last season.

"What kind of history?" Cap presses.

"The kind I'm not going to talk about."

Cap pinches the bridge of his nose. Panda fucking snickers. I glare at them.

"Listen, I'm handling it," I say.

Cap glares back while Panda shakes his head. "Just like you handled LA?" Cap tosses out.

Shit. So that's still a sore spot. While I was hoping the team had moved past it, it's clear that the bitter ending of last season is still sharp in everyone's, especially Austin's, mind.

Panda shoots me a sympathetic look. "You seem to get on all right with Jesse," he tosses out helpfully. "Does he know?" Or not helpful at all.

I shrug. "I don't know."

"Fuck," Austin groans. "Sims, we can't have this shit, tension, whatever, on the team. Make it right with Carpenter's sister. And make sure things stay right with him. Got it?"

"Yeah, of course," I agree, feeling Cap's disappointment like a punch to the gut. Why do I keep messing this up? How many chances am I going to get until there's none left? I stand from the bench and the guys shuffle back to give me space. "I'll fix it."

"Good," Austin says, clapping me on the back.

"See you on the ice," I toss over my shoulder as I leave the weight room.

Did Sofia tell Jesse that we hooked up? No, there's no way a sister would confide that shit in her brother. Oh, fuck. Did I just blow up her spot by being straight with Cap and Panda?

I groan, pinching the bridge of my nose. But I can't exactly lie to Austin, can I? Look how poorly that worked out for me in the past.

No, I need to put the team first. My career depends on it. Here, I'm Eddie Sims. Period. Sofia witnessed the lavish lifestyle my family leads. She saw my parents and Preston, but no one here knows who my family is.

I've never been open about them before. A handful of years ago, one of my father's hospitals came under review for insurance fraud. A man had lied about his daughter's symptoms, fudging some paperwork, to get her into a clinical trial. While my parents felt for the guy, and his daughter, the scheme threatened to ruin the reputation of the hospital, not to mention dilute the results of the trial. Since then, my parents began adopting a quieter relationship with the media, with the public. Then, my first real girlfriend, the one who flipped the universe upside down for me, made me believe in that glow that Preston and Heather have, tried to use my family's access and medical resources to supplement a prescription drug addiction I was too blind to catch.

Delphine broke my fucking heart. But more than that, she rattled my trust. She upended my desire to find a partner, one I could be fully honest with. One I could trust my family to know. I'd been taken advantage of for years—by friends, teachers, teammates—but Delphine was the final nail in the coffin.

Since her, it was easier to introduce myself as Eddie Sims, to live a separate public persona that wouldn't speak of Lance and Margaret Lawrence's legacy. But now that Sofia has met them, now that Preston has met her and Heather adores her, it seems silly. Living this double life. This lie.

If Jesse learns I hooked up with his sister, I'll deal with it. That, I can handle.

What I can't handle is how messed up I feel about Sofia being here. Because I can't stop thinking about her. I can't stop remembering how my name, my real name, sounded when it dropped from her lips.

Theo.

For the first time in years, I wish someone, other than my family, would call me Theo and see the real me. The way Sofia did, if only for a night.

I need to make things right with her. First, for the team. But also, for me.

THE OPPORTUNITY TO see Sofia again presents itself a few days later. It's the first weekend the whole team is back in Boston and a reunion is in order. Tonight, we're partying downtown at a club I used to frequent.

I text Jesse the info to meet but an hour before I swing by his place, he tells me he's feeling off.

Frowning, I tap out a message.

THEO

You okay? You need something?

JESSE

Got a fever and my ear's ringing.

THEO

Damn. Doctor?

JESSE

Appointment in the morning.

THEO

Good.

I pace the length of my living room, wondering if I should ask the next question. Will she shoot me down? Will Jesse even relay my message? Argh, I'm being a goddamn pussy.

THEO

If Sofia still wants to come out, I can pick her up and make sure she gets home okay.

JESSE

You can text her.

Before I tell him I don't have her number, he sends it.

Damn. Now what? Do I message her? If I don't, will Jesse tell her I chickened out?

Jesus, when did I become a prepubescent boy again? Sofia and I already hooked up. We've already exchanged heavy conversation. I've already pissed her the fuck off. I should be able to text her no problem.

I stop pacing and type a message.

THEO
I'm coming to pick you up in thirty.

SOFIA
Who is this?

THEO
Guess.

SOFIA
Eddie?

I snort. Damn, now that I told her to call me Theo, she definitely won't.

THEO
It's Theo. Still want to come out tonight?

SOFIA
Not with you.

THEO
I don't believe that.

SOFIA
[Middle finger emoji]

THEO
I still don't believe you. Besides, Claire asked if you were coming. All the girls will be there tonight...

SOFIA

So?

THEO

So, part of a do-over is making a social circle. We can leave whenever you want.

Three minutes tick by with no response. I resume my pacing, wondering if she's just going to blow me off. But then, my phone dings.

SOFIA

Give me twenty.

THEO

See you soon.

I drop my phone to the coffee table and grin. Tonight, I'll make things right with Sofia. Tonight, I'll be her friend and hopefully, she'll call me Theo again.

JESUS, she can call me whatever the fuck she wants. Because the moment Sofia answers the door to her brother's apartment, I'm speechless. As in, words can't form, thoughts don't compute.

"Theo?" The sweetest word, my real name, on the sweetest lips brings me back to reality.

"You look...Jesus, Sofia. You're gorgeous," I blurt out, with zero fucking chill.

One side of her mouth rolls upward, the tiniest bit, yet it feels like a win. I made her almost, kind-of, maybe smile. And I feel like I scored a goal at the buzzer.

"Thanks," she murmurs. "You ready to go?"

I gesture toward the hallway, and she steps out, locking the door behind her.

"How's your brother?" I ask.

"Sleeping. He feels terrible and I know he would have enjoyed tonight."

"I'm glad you decided to still come out."

"Yeah, well, I never say no to a good time," she says it coyly, as if she's insinuating something else, something more than tonight. I frown, not liking her blasé response. Is she suggesting that the night in Maui meant nothing? That she has a lot of nights like that, with other men? Or am I reading into this?

She smirks and I shake my head.

Sofia can pretend all she wants that she can't stand me, but when she looks at me, there's a heat in her gaze, a pull in her tone, that speaks to more than our one night in the past. Nope, there's something between us and even if I can't act on it, I sure as hell am going to make her admit it.

"But I'm better than a good time," I reply, half joking, half not. I lead her toward my SUV in the parking lot.

She snickers. "More lies you tell yourself?"

"If that's what you want to believe, sweetheart." I grin.

"Ugh." She rolls her eyes. "So generic. Sweetheart."

"Would *babe* be better?"

She gives me a dirty look. "Why are you smiling anyway?"

"Because I forgot how much I like being with you." I open the passenger door.

She narrows her eyes at me, dark with the slightest flare of curiosity. Good, I want to intrigue her; she sure as hell intrigues me. "I don't trust you."

"I know."

"I don't even like you."

"That's fine."

"So why are you still smiling?" she snaps, her tone filled with frustration I latch onto.

"Because you still want me."

She glowers, her hand lifting as if to smack me. But she holds back while a part of me wishes she'd let that palm fly. Let her passion escape since she's clearly holding so much back.

"I want you too, Sofia." I lower my voice, watch her pupils dilate. "And by the end of the night—"

"You think you'll have me?" she scoffs.

"No." I shake my head. "I think you may like me again." I tip my head toward the car seat, and she slips inside.

I wait until she's buckled in before shutting the door and rounding the SUV. My heartbeat is erratic, filled with an adrenaline that I usually experience on the ice.

I've been partying hard the past few seasons. I've hit up clubs across the country, taken shots at dive bars up and down the coasts, and ended nights with random women in random hotel rooms.

Tonight, I feel that zing that's been missing for too long. In fact, I don't remember the last time I felt it. The awareness, the expectation, the want and the chase and the moments. Each one infused with excitement and recklessness. I felt it with Sofia in Maui and now again.

Tonight isn't just about getting fucked up at a club and finding a hot woman to greet the morning with. No, tonight, I want to earn Sofia's attention, her desire. And I want to hear her cry out my name again.

CHAPTER 8
SOFIA

"I'm going to call you Theo," I decide when he starts the ignition and pulls out of Jesse's apartment complex.

"I'm happy to hear it."

"It's not about you. It's just that...from everything I learned, I think I'd dislike Eddie even more."

He chuckles, the sound low. Annoying. Jesus, what is it about this guy? I'm telling him I don't like him, I don't trust him, I don't want him and—well, that's the issue, isn't it? The only reason why Theodore Lawrence's lie hurt, is because I felt, *feel*, something for him. Something that stuck with me when I left Maui, something I still crave. His touch. His scent. His bedroom eyes and raspy voice.

I shift in my seat, my thighs rubbing together, as I turn to look out the window.

"I'd like to prove to you that you can trust me, that, despite all my fucked-up bullshit, I am an honest guy. Some may even argue too honest."

I scoff, although, deep down, a part of me believes him.

"I never promise roses and sunsets," he continues, explanation further. "I only promise the night. A good time."

"We already did that," I remind him.

"It was good, wasn't it?" He quirks an eyebrow, his gaze unsettling me before he turns to look back at the road. His palm slips across the top of the steering wheel and for a second, I remember what it felt like sliding up my spine. The way his fingers dipped between my thighs. His breath, panting, fanning out across my collarbone.

I clear my throat.

"It was," he says decisively, answering for me. But I can't deny it because…yeah, it fucking was. Theo undid me and then, he made me feel the same way Don did. Like a fool. Like someone he couldn't be completely honest with, even as I gave my confessions freely.

Knowing Theo lied hurt. It burned to realize that I trusted the wrong man. Again! It also forced me to admit that Don's dismissal wasn't a one-off, since something similar happened only a month later. Do I attract the wrong guys? A slew of memories, of one-night stands and sorority mixers, rolls through my mind. Or am I attracted to the wrong guys? Do I search out the reckless, passionate, exciting moments because I want to live in them so badly?

Unbidden, Theo reaches over and takes my hand. I flinch but he tightens his grip. "Give me a shot, Sof. Please. Even if you don't want anything to happen between us. Give me a shot to earn your trust, your respect."

"I don't have time to waste with people who aren't upfront with me from the start." Life's too short to take things for granted. I wasted too much time with Don, and I don't want to repeat that with Theo.

"I get that," he replies. "And I know I messed up, but I'm trying to be straight with you now. Listen, just have fun tonight. Enjoy yourself and let me be along for the ride."

What? I wait for him to say more. To make it about him or him and me but he just smiles wider.

"Dance with the girls. Take shots. Let yourself enjoy

tonight; enjoy Boston. For you. I swear I will be the perfect gentleman and see you home safely."

Dance. Shots. Have fun.

While I'm not a stranger to any of the above, particularly during my college years, it's been a different story since I became serious with Don. As my friend group shrunk, I grew guarded. And every time I've let that guard slip, it's cost me.

Something about Theo's expression tells me he's being sincere. Truthful. I don't know how I know this, but I do. Tonight, he's got my back. My shoulders drop and I relax into the seat. It's been a long time since anyone other than my brother has had my back.

And I want to believe him. I want it so badly that I tip my chin down and murmur, "Okay."

He squeezes my hand in confirmation before turning back to the road. We sit the rest of the ride in silence but it's not the same tense, awkward silence of earlier. Now, there's a thread of acceptance in the connection between us. There's an acknowledgment, an agreement, that didn't exist earlier. Tonight, I'm going to be a normal, twenty-four-year-old woman out with a group of friends. And Theo… Theo's going to be the guy trying to earn back my trust.

A tingle shoots down my spine because I really hope he does.

THE CLUB IS DARK, crowded, and hazy with smoke. It's the perfect backdrop for poor decisions, for those wishing to fall into obscurity and remain hidden until sunrise.

Another thrill rips through me as I clutch Theo's hand. He leads me through a mass of bodies until we arrive at a red velvet rope. The woman guarding the stairs to a VIP section recognizes him immediately.

"Eddie, long time, baby. How've you been?" She kisses him hello with a familiarity I dislike.

He's perfectly polite as he flashes a grin. "Good, thanks. Team up there?"

"Yes. Your table's on the right." She unhooks the rope to let us pass. Her gaze rolls over me but not with the judgment I anticipated. More as if she's weighing if I'm worthy enough for Theo.

Strange.

Theo and I climb the staircase and when we enter the VIP section, a cheer rings out.

"There he is!" Panda points at him. "And…is that Ms. Sofia Carpenter?"

I grin, unable to keep up my aloofness in the presence of Luca Pandatelli. He's much too likable to fake it around and I'm already caving. I lift my hand in a little wave.

"You know what this means." Panda holds his arms out, spinning to look at the rest of the guys and their girls.

"Shots!" Claire fist pumps the air.

Easton groans and Abbi grins.

Theo's fingers find the small of my back and he shifts me forward, toward the team. Everyone is already lining up at the bar while a bartender fills shot glasses with chilled Patron.

"Happy you came out." Claire kisses my cheek hello.

"It's nice to be out again!" another beautiful blonde exclaims, her palm pressing into the slight swell of her abdomen. "But I'm not sure how long I'm going to make it. Truth, these pregnancy hormones are wiping me out." She glances at me. "Hey, I'm Vivi."

"Who works at the women's shelters," I blurt out.

Her smile grows. "Yes! Are you thinking of volunteering?"

"I am. I'm signed up for some events at Mass General—"

"With Maybelle's House?"

"Yes! Next month."

"Oh my gosh! Thank you so much!" Vivi does a little dance, clasping my hand.

"I'm Sofia, Jesse's sister."

"Of course. It's good to meet you. I'd love to introduce you to some of the projects I'm working on if female empowerment is your thing." She passes me a shot glass and picks up a glass of water for herself.

I bite my bottom lip. "Always interested. But my passions lie with the hospital and the prisons."

Vivi grins, as if my answer pleases her. "Personal connections?"

"Yes," I say, not sharing that my father is an ex-con. "I just started at the prison this week and I've already made a friend," I continue. "His name is Sam and he's hoping to earn his GED before his release in a few months."

"That's awesome. Those with a personal connection make the best volunteers. You give from your heart. If you'd like to dip your toes into some of the work at women's shelters, I'd be happy to show you around."

"Yeah, I'd like that." I turn toward Theo, surprised to see him empty-handed. "Where's your tequila?"

He shakes his head. "I'm driving you home tonight, remember?"

"You can have a drink," I say, surprised that he'd forgo alcohol when I remember how fond he is of libations.

"Not when I'm responsible for precious cargo." He gestures to the bartender and orders a club soda.

I frown, his words washing over me. If another guy, say Don, said them, I'd wonder what he was playing at. There would be an angle, a fallout that would somehow blow back on me. But Theo's tone wasn't flippant or annoyed; it was sincere. He's not going to drink tonight, the first night his team is all together to kick off the new season, because he's driving me home.

Clearly, he's just being responsible and yet…his actions affect me. Because we could always Uber home or catch a ride or call Jesse. But Theo wants to prove himself to me and right now, he's doing that. He's showing me that he can be responsible instead of reckless, honest instead of shady.

"Cheers, girl!" Claire appears, clinking her glass against mine. She wraps an arm around Vivi's shoulders and speaks to her belly. "Let your mama dance for one hour before she passes out with exhaustion."

Vivi laughs.

I toss back the tequila, savoring the slow burn as it trails down my throat. A lime appears before me, as Theo holds it out. Slowly, I part my lips and he places the lime between them, his gaze holding mine. I bite into the tart fruit, sucking on it for one blink, before Theo pulls it back and discards it on the top of the bar.

The corner of his mouth pulls into a lazy smile but his eyes blaze, hot and heady.

"I love this song!" Vivi announces, gripping Claire's arm.

"Good!" Claire shimmies. "Let's go dance."

Claire hooks her arm with mine and pulls me toward the dance floor. I glance over my shoulder, my eyes finding Theo's. But he smiles, posting up against the bar like there's nowhere else he'd rather be.

"Have fun," he mouths.

I nod, realizing just how much he wants me to enjoy tonight. To make friends, to settle in Boston. So I embrace the moment, immerse myself in it.

For the first time in a long time, I have real fun with girls I want to be my real friends.

CHAPTER 9
THEO

"You sick, bro?" Panda asks me.

"What? No." I shake my head, my gaze still trained on Sofia. Christ, can she move. The way her hips roll to the beat, her perfect ass taunting the shit out of me. Her curves, sexy and on display, making my—

"You're seriously not drinking?" Yaeger narrows his eyes.

I glare at him, annoyed that he interrupted my slow, sweet-as-fuck perusal of Sofia's delicious body. "No. I'm DD tonight."

"Since when has that ever stopped you?" Yaeger questions.

Panda grins. "He brought Sofia Carpenter."

"Why the hell do you keep saying her whole name?" I ask, turning to look at him.

Panda shrugs and chuckles. "I don't know. It's…catchy. Sounds like an actress or some shit."

I roll my eyes.

"You like her," Yaeger says like it's common knowledge.

"Of course I like her. She's Jesse's sister," I mutter.

Panda and Yaeger burst into laughter. The annoying kind

that causes grandpas to slap their knees and hockey players in their late twenties, early thirties to toss their heads back and nearly howl. Jesus.

"Holy fucking shit," Panda bites out, garnering Easton and Austin's attention. "You really like her, bro."

I take a swig of my club soda. No way am I admitting that I more than like Sofia. Or that I fucked her hard in Maui and she struck me senseless. No way am I admitting anything but—

"Your silence says it all." Yaeger whistles. He clasps my shoulder. "Good for you, Eddie. She's a good girl."

"You just met her," I point out.

"Vivi likes her; I can tell," he declares.

I drain my club soda. How did I end up with these guys as my closest friends? And what does it say that my closest friends still don't know my real name? Or shit about my family? What does it mean that Sofia, the woman who told me she doesn't even like me two hours ago, knows me better than anyone else in this room?

It's a sobering thought, but since I'm already sober, it depresses me more than anything. Maybe Preston was right; maybe I do need to let people in.

As the guys continue to joke at my expense, my gaze finds Sofia on the dance floor. She's carefree, laughing and dancing with Chloe, Claire, and Vivi. She's relaxed, having shed some of the armor she shields herself in around me. She's beautiful and I realize just how much I want her to know me. How much I want her to trust me. How much I want *her*.

I gesture that I'll take another club soda.

"Easy champ or they'll kick in," Panda jokes.

"You do right by her, she'll come around," Easton mutters, offering the only sensible advice I've heard tonight. "She keeps looking at you too."

I frown, my gaze darting back to the dance floor. Sure

enough, Sofia is staring right at me. But she doesn't look away. I don't know if it's the buzz from the alcohol, or the atmosphere of the club, or if she really does want me the way I crave her, but she holds my eyes. Her lips part and she turns toward me, beckoning me closer, inviting me to dance.

I don't give a shit that most of my team is watching. I place down my club soda and walk toward the woman I'm desperate to claim. I step right into her space and look at her hard, trying to gauge how drunk she is.

Her palms slide up, settling on my chest. Chloe, Claire, and Vivi read the room and give us a hell of a lot more space.

"How many shots did you take?" I ask.

Her palms slip down to the waistband of my jeans and curl around my hips. "Not nearly as many in Maui."

"This isn't Maui."

"I know," she breathes out.

"What do you want, Sofia?"

She gives me that subtle almost smile again. "You still owe me a dance."

I snort but acquiesce. We never did get our dance at Preston's wedding. That one would have been elegant and formal. That night was...so much more than a singular moment. Gathering her up in my arms, I give her the dance she's asking for. I waltz her around the space, careful to keep some distance between us, careful not to step over any lines. The dance is all fucking wrong for the music and I'm sure my teammates think I've lost my mind.

But Sofia cracks a smile. A real one. And then, a laugh.

We dance and spin and laugh like two kids who forgot how to have fun. Like two strangers who want to connect. Like two adults a little bit broken from our pasts trying to glue it all back together.

And this time, when our eyes hold, hers twinkle with something akin to like.

GETTING a tipsy Sofia home is a hell of a lot more fun than if she was any other woman. Instead of being sloppy and annoying, she's witty and truthful. I pick up each truth she drops, trying to piece together the puzzle that is Sofia Carpenter.

"I bolted because I liked you. That night…" She trails off, gripping the side mirror of my SUV to steady herself. She drops her head to her hand. "When I saw you in the magazine, saw your name, your team, I felt stupid. And at that moment, in Maui, I was still moving past the last guy who made me feel dumb." Her words are hushed, cloaked in a vulnerability she's rarely showed.

Something about it, her posture, her tone, causes my stomach to knot. I hate that I hurt her, made her doubt herself and her judgment. And I hate that I know Sofia isn't the first woman I made feel like this. I never lied; I never cheated. But I sure as fuck never gave a shit either. Not since Delphine…

"Hey." I step closer to Sofia. My palm rests across the small of her back. Dipping my head closer to hers, I murmur, "You're not stupid, babe. And I swear to you, I'm not Don."

She hiccups and shakes her head. Lifting her eyes to mine, they swim with heartache that horrifies me. Does she still love him? "That's the thing. I knew that. I knew it from the moment I met you and somehow, you not being upfront hurt worse than him. What does that mean, Theo? That I was more affected by you giving me the wrong name the night we met than I was by my ex-fiancé casting me aside because he learned that…"

"He learned what?" I press.

Horror washes over her face, draining it of color. Then she

bursts out a snort of laughter, shaking her head. "I drank too much."

"I like when you're truthful."

She quirks an eyebrow.

"I didn't really lie, babe," I remind her.

"Whatever."

"What did Don learn?" I ask again.

She sighs, "That my dad…a long time ago, he went to prison."

So not what I was expecting. "Okay," I say slowly.

"Okay? That's it?" she demands, her eyes narrowed.

I shrug. "Do you want to tell me why?"

"He did something wrong, he did. But he did it for the right reasons," she murmurs, as if wanting me to know her dad isn't an awful person.

Growing up in the world I was raised in, I know firsthand everything isn't always as it seems. Sometimes, good people do bad things. Sometimes, bad people are celebrated for doing bad things. Nothing is black and white.

"I'm not judging you, Sof," I tell her.

Her expression relaxes slightly. "He's still my dad."

"You're supposed to love your father. If he's given you a reason to, a real reason, then you're better off than lots of people whose dads have never been to prison."

She smiles. A real one. "I think so too." Her smile slips. "But Don felt his past was too much of a liability. That his family's connection to mine would result in too much negative press if anyone learned—"

"Hold up," I interject. "Douchebag Don told you he couldn't marry you because years ago, your dad got locked up?"

She nods.

I frown, trying to read between the lines. Something doesn't add up. "Didn't he know that your dad was in prison?"

She shakes her head. "His parents hired a PI."

My eyebrows lift. But after meeting the Servinos, I'm not surprised. They seem the type to cover their asses from any type of liability.

"I never told him," Sofia continues. Her gaze softens when it lands on mine. "What does it mean that I never told him? Not in the entire year we were together. And I told you…after knowing you for what? A handful of hours?"

"It means you trust me, Sofia," I spell it out for her. Because while she keeps spouting off that she doesn't like me or trust me, she's lying if she thinks there isn't something between us. This pull, a magnetism, a chemistry that's potent and…real.

"No bullshit," she whispers.

"None. Tell me."

She wrinkles her nose. "I like you, Theo. And it scares me because sometimes, I think I'm not a good judge of character. I trust too easily, fall too fast. I like to live in the moment, experience it all, everything. And with you…I can already tell the fallout will hurt more than with Don."

Damn. When Sofia Carpenter goes in, she goes all in.

I clear my throat and take her hands. "No bullshit."

She regards me cautiously.

"I like you too. More than I've liked a woman, any woman, in a long-ass time. When I was in college, I fell in love for the first time. A woman named Delphine who straight up ruled my heart. I did every cliché thing in the book—blew off my friends, fucked up shit with my team, and did her bidding."

Sofia narrows her eyes, not liking this story. Or maybe this version of me. In hindsight, I don't much care for it either.

"You know my family. You are the only person connected to the Hawks, save for Coach and members of senior management, who know the truth about the Lawrence family."

"What about them?" she asks.

"Babe, my family is fucking loaded."

She laughs. "Yeah, I got that."

"That's why I go by Eddie Sims."

"Right. But what's that have to do with the girl from college?"

"Delphine. I'll give you the Cliff's Notes version. Delphine learned of my family's connections, especially with hospitals and pharmacies. My dad is a shareholder in several private hospitals in the country and has a lot of pull with doctors and pharmacists."

A strange look ripples over Sofia's face but she doesn't say anything, so I continue.

"Anyway, she used those connections, leveraged my family name, to further her prescription drug habit."

Sofia sucks in a sharp breath, horrified.

"I know," I agree. "It fucking broke me because—"

"You trusted her."

"Implicitly. I loved her. Meanwhile, she was making connections through my phone, using the Lawrence name, to get fucked up. When all was said and done, my father was furious and I had to work to pay back all the drugs she got that she never paid for, saying I would."

Sofia groans. "Oh Theo, that's, that's awful. Evil."

"Yeah," I agree. "So we have more in common than you realize. I know what it's like to feel naive and used. I never meant to make you feel that way, ever."

She must read something in my expression because she raises her hand and places it against my cheek. "It hurts, doesn't it? To be made a fool?"

"Yes."

"I believe you. I believe that you weren't trying to mislead me that night," she says softly.

I grin, relief mixing with hope in my stomach. "Does this mean you like me again?"

She chuckles. "I never truly stopped liking you. I just

wanted to *not* like you. But even then, I still enjoyed the attention you gave me."

The confession rocks through me, the best thing I've heard all night.

"Then I'll be sure to lavish it on you."

She snorts.

I wrap my arm more firmly around her waist to steady her. "But not tonight, sweet Sofia. Tonight, I need to take you home so you can get your beauty rest. Nurse your hangover in the morning."

She giggles and allows me to help her into the SUV. When I reach over to grab her seat belt and buckle her in, she takes hold of my wrist. I turn toward her, our faces so close that we're breathing in each other's exhales.

"Thank you for tonight, Theo."

"It was nothing."

"No, it was something. You know that." Her eyes search mine, as if needing confirmation.

"Yes. It was something."

I grin and she smiles back.

"I hated knowing that I hurt you, Sof. It was never my intention. I've made a lot of mistakes, but I don't want to make them with you."

She draws in a sharp breath, her thumb pressing into the pulse point on my wrist.

"I don't want to make them with you, either."

"Good." I brush a kiss over her cheek. "Then we won't."

She turns her head, our noses touch, and the moment stretches, shimmering with expectation.

"I need to take you home now," I say, forcing the words out when dropping Sofia back at Jesse's is the last fucking thing I want to do.

"Okay," she agrees.

I close the passenger door, round the SUV, and turn on the

ignition. Sofia and I ride the drive back to her brother's in silence but it's comfortable. It's filled with an understanding, a realization, that we're not as different as we once thought.

That we may even be more alike than we want to admit.

CHAPTER 10
SOFIA

"What time did you leave the club last night?" Claire asks as we sit down to lunch.

We're at a cute little salad bar and even though the weather is cooling off, we opted to sit outside.

Claire tucks her hair behind her ears as she raises her eyebrows at me.

"A little after you and Easton." I stab my straw into my sparkling water, more hungover than I care to admit. Mostly because I drank too much vodka and tequila but also, a part of me is still reeling from being so honest with Theo. Wasn't my experience with Don a cautionary tale? Aren't I supposed to be taking a break from men?

But then why does being with Theo feel so right? And isn't this a rationalization I've fed myself for years? Feeling confused and out of sorts, I'm relieved when Chloe shows up, wearing a baseball cap and sunglasses.

She plops down in the chair between Claire and me with a massive coffee. "The light hurts."

I crack a grin as Claire chuckles.

"I'm with you, Chloe," I say.

"I haven't had that much tequila in ages. I blame it all on Panda," she continues.

I nod in agreement.

Claire shakes her head and takes a bite of her salad. "You guys are lightweights." She turns her attention toward me. "Did Eddie take you home?"

"Yeah. He was a perfect gentleman." I chew another bite of my salad and push the breadbasket toward Chloe. She shoots me a grateful look and swipes a roll.

"Abbi has some youth outreach events coming up too. I think they're all at local high schools if you're interested?" Claire asks me.

"I'd love to check them out." I take a long drink of my water, relieved that it dulls some of the throb in my head. "But my schedule is filling up. One of the men I'm helping at the prison, Sam, is studying to get his GED before he's released in a few months. I've agreed to spend more time making sure he's prepared for the exam."

"That's really nice of you, Sofia," Claire smiles. "Abbi always has events so it's an open invitation."

"There's some type of outreach every month," Chloe agrees.

"My favorite events are the ones held at gyms so we can try out some classes," Claire laughs.

"Oh! That reminds me." I dig into my purse and pull out a flyer that caught my eye this morning. "Do you girls want to sign up for pole dancing?"

Chloe freezes, her sunglasses sliding down her nose as she peers at me. Claire's eyes widen before she bursts into laughter. "You're serious?"

I shrug, passing her the flyer. "Sure, why not? It looks like great exercise and a hell of a lot of fun."

Chloe points between us as Claire reads over the flyer. "The two of you together is bad news."

"Or the best thing ever," Claire shoots back. Her smile widens. "I'm so in! Easton will love/hate this idea."

I chuckle. "I'll sign us up. You want in?" I ask Chloe.

She shakes her head, pushing her glasses back up on her nose. "I'm not brave enough for that."

"Oh please, you took my brother to a wedding to show up your ex-fiancé. You're definitely brave enough to pole dance." Claire turns to me. "Sign us all up. I'll ask Indy too. She's in wedding planning mode and needs an intervention."

"Ex-fiancé?" I ask Chloe sympathetically. "You have one of those too?"

Chloe laughs before nodding. "At the time it was devastating but not marrying Steven turned out to be the best decision I've ever made."

I nod, biting my bottom lip. "I definitely dodged a bullet too," I offer, smiling at my friends. It's nice to have my own outlet, instead of an extension of my boyfriend's. While I know the girls are friends with Theo, I think they're sincere in their friendship with me.

"So pole dancing is a go. Is there anything else we can help with as you settle in Boston? You mentioned going back to school?" Chloe asks slowly.

"I keep thinking about it."

"For nursing, right?" Claire asks.

I shrug. "I was in the nursing program. I thought about medical school but to be honest, there's so much I want to do. Being a doctor, you're always on call. You practically live at the hospital."

"You could do family medicine," Claire points out.

"Yeah, but I wouldn't."

The girls laugh.

I smile and shake my head, arching my neck so they can see my scar. "I had leukemia as a kid."

Claire murmurs something softly, moving closer to trace my scar with her eyes. "Battle scars."

"Something like that," I agree.

"I'm sorry, Sofia," Chloe says. "I can't even, I can't imagine."

"It was really tough on…well, my whole family."

"But you're okay now?" Claire asks.

"So far, so good," I say. I can never bring myself to admit that I'm cured because there's always a thought in the back of my mind, a little reminder of what was and what could be again.

"Is that why you volunteer at hospitals so much?" Chloe asks, putting it all together.

"Yes."

"And the prisons?" Chloe tilts her head, studying me. But she doesn't ask it in a nosy, judgey way. Nope, she seems genuinely curious, as if she's certain there's a real reason, rooted in a logical explanation. And there is.

"My dad," I admit, feeling safe to speak about him when I usually shut down any conversation that gets too close to the truth. It's almost like Theo's reaction last night gave me the permission, the confidence, to be honest. "He was incarcerated for five years. He's been out about six years now. He lives in New Hampshire. But his time in prison... There are a lot of programs. I mostly do tutoring, helping inmates get their GED, like Sam, or even college degrees."

"Wow," Chloe says slowly. "Do you see him a lot?"

"Not really," I admit. "We talk all the time, but I haven't visited him in ages. He likes to keep his life quiet and simple now. But, since we're so close in Boston, I think I'll see him more frequently."

"That would be nice," Claire offers. "Boston isn't nearly as far as Maui."

I laugh. "Exactly."

"Were you close, when you were a kid?" Chloe asks.

"Very. We still are. But before, he wasn't so guarded. Now, he doesn't like to travel much, he just sticks to his daily routine. When I was little, we used to spend summers at a lake house at Mille Lacs Lake, in Minnesota." I bite my lip, remembering those carefree, joyful summer days. "When he went away, I used to write him letters, all the time. And he would write me back stories, intricate ones with world-building and multiple characters arcs. They were the best. Once he was released, I think he struggled to fit back into society. He moved to New Hampshire. A friend there hooked him up with a mechanic job. By then, Mom was married to Jesse's dad, Mitch, and I was older. Everyone kind of had their own lives, you know?"

"Yeah," Claire says, her expression sympathetic. "Still must be hard not seeing him as much as you'd like."

"It is. That's kind of why the volunteering stuck. When I help the other inmates, in a way, it feels like I'm helping him."

"That makes sense," Chloe says.

"Well, if you need anyone to tag along on your volunteering, let me know," Claire offers.

"Me too." Chloe lifts her hand.

"Thanks. I will," I say, surprised that I mean it. I haven't had a real girlfriend, a confidant, in so long, it's invigorating to find I have a genuine connection with Claire and Chloe.

We finish our lunch, talk about random things pertaining to the team or our families, and hug goodbye. When I get home, I see a note on the kitchen table, in handwriting I don't recognize.

Sof,

Here's Indy's number. She's a professor at Brighton. Give her a ring if you have any questions about admissions. Let me know how else I can help. Whatever you need, babe, I'm here.

Theo

I grin, snatching up the paper napkin and hugging it to my chest.

"Jesse? You here?" I call out, peeking into his bedroom.

I know he had a doctor's appointment this morning, but I thought he'd be home by now.

I enter my bedroom and collapse on the bed, the exhaustion from a night of partying catching up with me. Staring at my ceiling, I wonder how I already feel more at home in Boston than I did in Michigan. Or Maui.

How have I already found friends here when I couldn't connect with anyone in my hometown? Why did it take this long for me to realize how small I've made my circle?

My phone beeps with a message and I pick it up, holding it over my face.

DAD

Hey Sofie girl, sorry I missed your call. Let's catch up this week.

SOFIA

No worries. Can't wait to talk.

DAD

You like Boston?

SOFIA

Very much.

DAD

Good. I'm happy to hear it.

I send him a heart emoji and am about to place my phone down when another message comes through.

JESSE

Hey, Sims took me to see the doctor. Appointment went okay. Picked up antibiotics. We're at Easton's house, watching some game tape now. You good?

SOFIA

Yeah. Feel better.

JESSE

I'll bring home dinner.

SOFIA

Okay. Thanks.

I move to place my phone down again when a new message beeps. I chuckle to myself.

THEO

Don't listen to Jesse. He's so exhausted, he won't make it till dinner. Let me take you out.

I smile at the words, a flicker of hope running through me. For all my tough talk, I desperately want to say yes. So I do.

SOFIA

Okay.

THEO

That's it? You're not going to gush about how excited you are to see me two nights in a row?

SOFIA

I thought you were being a perfect gentleman? Gentlemen don't call women out.

THEO

That was last night. I wanted you to like me again and you said you do.

SOFIA

And tonight?

THEO

...

My heart rate ticks up, and I find myself enjoying this little banter we've got going on.

SOFIA

...

THEO

Tonight, I make you want me. Because Sof, I haven't stopped thinking about you.

Damn. Theo Lawrence has game.

But, even though my heart is racing and my body suddenly feels warmer than a moment ago, I have the good sense to play it cool. Coy.

SOFIA

We'll see, Theo.

He responds a second later.

THEO

We will.

I let out a breathless laugh, his words coated in challenge. In determination. We both know if Theo puts his mind to it, I'll be begging for his touch during the appetizer. Because I haven't forgotten how his hands feel on my body or the way he made me feel more in one kiss than Don did during our entire eight-month stay in Maui.

But Theo? Theo doesn't need a backdrop to woo because he's intoxicating all on his own. And tonight, I'll find out just how much.

I'm going to need a nap for this.

I chuckle to myself and finally drop my phone to my side. Then, I close my eyes and sleep off my hangover in preparation of tonight.

Because I know that Theodore Lawrence is bringing his A game. There's no question that I'll want him, mostly because I've never stopped, but also because I'll be powerless against his sincere apologies, skilled mouth, and incredibly capable hands.

CHAPTER 11
THEO

I'm nervous. More nervous than I've been around a woman in a long time. After rinsing off, I take time shaving, fixing my hair, being a huge douchebag and posing in front of the mirror to make sure my biceps still pop. They do.

But yeah, don't ever admit that to anyone. Ever.

I bite down on my toothbrush and stare at myself. I'm not trying to sound like a dick by saying I look good but...I look good. And not good in a he-knows-how-to-dress-and-has-that-swagger way. Good as in healthy. I look healthy...happy. Gone is the strung-out, haggard look I was starting to cop from too many late nights partying. The bags under my eyes have disappeared. My skin looks better. Even my eyes are... brighter. Huh.

Is this because I've spent the summer working my ass off to up my game for this season? Is this because I've cut back severely on my social outings? Or is this because Sofia has injected my life with a lightness that didn't previously exist? Whatever it is, maybe a combination of all three, I like instead of loathe what I see in the mirror.

My phone rings and I startle, blinking away the cloud of thoughts.

"Hey, Pres," I answer.

"Theo, how are you?" My brother's warm voice rolls through the line and I grin.

"Better than you if you're calling from your honeymoon."

He laughs. "Fuck off."

"How's Heather?"

"Great. We just got to Santa Margherita Ligure this morning."

I let out a whistle, setting the phone to speaker to comb my hair. "Look at you. And here, I thought you'd certainty stay in Portofino."

"You know how Heather prefers the more local, understated places."

I grin. I do know. It's one of the things I love most about my sister-in-law. She can take tea with the cream of the crop in London society and still feel at home in dusty sandals and a backpack, exploring. Or, in this case, sunbathing at an Italian seaside destination among the locals. "Yeah, she's the best."

"She is." A note of pride hangs in my brother's tone.

"Happy for you, man."

"Me too. So how are you?"

I bark out a laugh. "You're calling me from Italy to see how I'm doing? What's up, Pres?"

My brother chuckles. "I just spoke to Mom. She mentioned something about you having a date…with a girl named *Sofia*."

I laugh again, knowing that oversharing with Mom was going to come back and bite me in the ass. Not that I wouldn't tell Preston, but clearly, he's already put two and two together.

"Would this happen to be wedding coordinator Sofia?" He practically sing-songs, much too excited for a simple date.

But I play along. "It would."

He whistles. "She lives in Boston? What are the odds?"

"She recently moved here. Actually, after she gave me the slip the next morning—"

My brother laughs, enjoying that detail a little too much as I fill him in.

"And now, her stepbrother is my new teammate," I finish.

Preston swears. "Seriously? That's—"

"Crazy?" I supply.

"Fate," he counters, a romantic at heart.

Now it's my turn to laugh. Because I don't believe in things like fate and destiny. Right?

"That's really cool that you reconnected. The morning of my wedding, you had that look again."

"What look?" I wonder, wanting to know exactly what I portrayed after my night with Sofia. Being with her made me feel invincible again, like I was flying, like I could achieve anything. Did Preston see that too?

"Captivated. Like something yanked you out of the aloof, uninterested demeanor you use to keep women at bay."

I jerk back and stare at the phone. Is that how I live my life? Is that how my family views my relationships?

"Pres, man, I never—"

"I'm not saying it to be a dick or dredge up shit from the past. I'm saying it so you know that after you met Sofia, you looked and acted a hell of a lot happier and engaged with the world, our world, than usual. Where are you going for dinner?"

"Just a downtown spot. The Ivy."

"Well, have fun. If you want to analyze every detail tomorrow, give me a call."

I bark out a laugh. Yeah, guilty. I totally did that shit with Delphine a million moons ago. Truth be told, I was worse than a girl. "Thanks, Pres. Tell Heather hello."

"Will do. 'Bye."

I hang up the phone and stand in front of my closet, staring at the rows of black and blue jeans, designer sweaters, and posh boots and lace-up shoes. As much as I distance myself from my previous life, the fashion part, of looking good, presentable, at all times, stayed with me.

I dress quickly, in a white button-down shirt with the sleeves rolled up. I pull a trendy vest over it, giving an edgier look than I usually rock around town. A pair of jeans with some rips throughout and dress shoes. It's straddling the line of posh and edgy, which somehow seems symbolic of my life, but I don't want to think about that too much.

I swipe up a leather jacket and leave my condo. Tonight, I'm not going to second-guess myself. I'm not going to be the Eddie Boston fans love to hate. Or, for some of the women, hate to love. I don't want to be the obnoxious party guy who fucked up last season and hurt my teammates in the process.

No, now I'm the guy trying to win back the trust of Sofia Carpenter. And tonight, that's more than enough.

Because Sofia makes me feel like me again. She makes me want more than a fleeting night, than a drunken encounter. She pushes me to be better, to strive for more, to grow up a bit.

I never realized I wanted any of those damn things but with her, I want them all.

"YOU'RE EARLY," she says when she pulls open the door.

My mouth goes dry as I suddenly forget how to breathe. Her dark hair is curled in loose waves, wrapping around her shoulders, and trailing down her back. Her dark eyes are smoky, her lashes thick, sexy as sin. And her lips, instead of the red slash I expected, her lips are a dusty rose. Soft, inviting, innocent in a way the rest of her look isn't.

Sofia is rocking a leather mini skirt with over-the-knee

boots and a thin sweater that clings to her breasts. It hangs off one shoulder, tempting as hell.

I clear my throat. "You look…you are beautiful, Sofia Carpenter."

A slow smile spreads across her lips. A real one. Not that hesitant maybe crap but a true, genuine smile that lights her face up and makes me fall just a little more in like with her.

"You clean up well too, Theo."

I hold out my hand. "Ready?"

She crosses the threshold and places her palm in mine. "Ready."

"Where's Jesse?" I ask, worried that he'll be pissed I'm taking his sister out again. I need to get on the same page with him but…how can I when things with Sofia are so new? It's only our first date.

"He's out tonight. Met a lady friend." Sofia rolls her eyes. "Those antibiotics kicked in fast."

I chuckle.

"He won't be home till tomorrow," she tacks on.

"He's a true teammate," I joke, knowing he wouldn't see it that way if he knew I was planning to get serious with his sister. I wait for her to lock up and try real damn hard not to check out her ass. But fuck, if it's not perfectly round in that leather skirt.

As I lead Sofia toward my SUV, a thrill moves through me. Tonight, I'm starting a new beginning. A fresh start with a woman who's quickly redefining the game for me.

CHAPTER 12
SOFIA

"You trying to wine and dine me, Theo?" I ask playfully over the top of my menu.

The restaurant we're at, The Ivy, is swanky. It's elegant and fancy and one of the most coveted places to dine at in Boston. At least, that's what my Google search told me.

I have no idea how Theo managed to snag reservations so last minute, but I'd be lying if I didn't admit that I feel special he put the extra time in to take me someplace nice. Not that I need nice and fancy. But I do need knowing I'm a priority. That I matter. Right now, Theo is checking that box with a big tick.

"I'm trying to woo you, Sofia," he replies, winking.

Is it lame that even his cheesy lines make my heart rate increase? Probably. Ugh, why do I always do this? I fall back into old patterns so easily. Too easily. But as I study Theo, the soft glow of candlelight rippling over his features, I can tell he's trying. That he wants tonight to go well. That this isn't just a date but *the* date.

The realization shuts down my wayward thoughts and I lean closer to him, noting how his eyes widen. "It's working, isn't it?" he tosses out, clinging to that swagger he naturally exudes.

I pick up my wineglass and take a slow sip. "What do you think?"

He grins. "I think you're better at this than I am."

I laugh. "Better at what?"

"Life. Dating. Whatever you want to call this." He gestures between us.

"What would you call this?" I quirk an eyebrow. Inside, my heart thuds and nerves rattle around. But I play it cool because if there's one thing I perfected with all my failed non-relationships it's never let them see you sweat.

"The best first date I've ever been on." His answer is sincere, at odds with his wisecracking ass. It causes my heart to melt and some of my nerves to still.

"Mine too," I say softly.

Theo lifts his wineglass and clinks it against mine. "To tonight."

"Tonight," I echo, taking another sip of my wine.

We order our entrees and while I worried our conversation would feel forced, especially since we already slept together, things flow naturally between us.

"Thanks for sharing Indy's number. We're going to get together for lunch. She was so gracious and offered to meet."

"All the BHH women are awesome," Theo says slowly. "For the longest time, I didn't get it. Didn't understand how the guys on my team would want to lock themselves down like that but..." He shakes his head, his eyes filled with emotions. "I think I'm starting to."

Good Lord, does he have to be sweet on top of everything else?

"It's not always like that," I say softly.

"No, it's not," he agrees. "It's only when it's the right people, the right time...like this." He picks up his wineglass and flashes me that smirk before taking a sip. "Did you check out Brighton's admissions? What program were you in before?"

I sigh, toying with my napkin. I haven't told Jesse or my parents yet but, what's the harm in telling Theo? I'd love someone to weigh in and I know if nothing else, he'll be honest. "I was in a nursing program but I'm thinking of switching things up. Instead of nursing, I'm thinking about a degree in criminal justice."

He pulls back in surprise, his eyes narrowing to see if I'm serious. When he realizes I am, he doesn't toss out a bunch of criticisms or judgments like my family will. I'm sure they won't mean it in the long run, but their knee-jerk reaction will be to ask why I'd want to start over when I'm already three years into my nursing degree. They'll ask if I've thought this through or made the decision on a whim. "Because of your dad?"

"Yeah." I bite my lower lip. "When I started at college, I was thinking about philosophy. But then Don pointed out how impractical it is and nursing seemed like a more logical fit. But I never felt the same spark at the clinicals as I do when I'm volunteering. The prisons, working with inmates, that where I feel the most alive."

"Then why go back to school at all?"

I roll my eyes. "I have to earn some money to live."

He blushes, as if catching on that not everyone comes from a lush background. "Right. But what made you choose nursing to begin with? Why was that the logical choice?"

"I went into it because of my past and—"

"What past?" His eyebrows furrow together, low over his eyes.

Shit. "This isn't really a first date chat."

Theo's eyes soften. "In a lot of ways, we're past a first date. If you don't want to tell me, I get it. But if you do, I'm here to listen."

Of course he is. Jeez, where was Theo before I met Don? I

shake the thought from my head and take a deep breath. "When I was a kid, I had leukemia."

He pulls back, his face stricken. "Cancer."

"Yeah."

"But you're okay now? You're better."

I hesitate.

"Sofia?" Alarm threads through Theo's tone.

"Right now, I'm fine. I guess that's the thing with cancer. Even when you're cleared—five years in remission—the worry that it will reappear always hangs over you. Like a thundercloud threatening to burst."

Theo reaches across the table and takes my hand in his, loosely hanging onto my fingers. "That's why you volunteer at hospitals so much."

"Yes. I like the galas and fancy events best, the ones where they even invite the patients. A few have centered on pediatric oncology and those are my favorite. They make the kids so excited. Such special events to dress up and…pretend for a while that the thundercloud isn't raining on your head."

Grief spills across Theo's face, a deep understanding coloring his eyes more green than blue. "So, nursing called to you."

"I guess," I say. "I never gave it much thought. Mom suggested it, Don thought it was a good choice, so I did it. But I *feel* differently at the prisons. More passionate about supporting the inmates. I *want* to be part of criminal justice reform."

"Wow," he murmurs, tightening his hold on my fingers. "You gut me, Sofia Carpenter."

"How's that?"

"Most people spend their whole lives looking for something that speaks to them. Searching for something they can pour their passion, pieces of themselves into. For me, it's always been hockey. I've always known it, was fortunate to grow up with the support behind me, and dove right in. But

I've also always known it's not the norm. But you, you have so much good, light, passion, that there are endless things you can do and achieve. I think you could live to three hundred and still feel like you ran out of time."

The corners of my mouth curl. "You hit the nail on the head, Theo. Time is the greatest luxury, the most important gift, the only thing that truly matters, and most people take it all for granted. Not all the time, but too much of the time."

"I think I was one of those people, Sofia."

I shake my head. "But I don't think you are anymore."

He smirks again, that sexy grin that mixes sly with sincere. "I'm learning."

"I'm glad."

"Well, as far as I know, Brighton has a criminal justice program."

"I saw that. I'll learn more when I meet with Indy."

"Good," he says, and I can tell he means it. Theo is happy for me to follow my heart, wherever it leads.

He's quiet for a long moment and then, "We're more alike than you think."

"I'm beginning to see that." I mean it too. In Maui, I thought Theo and I came from two different worlds, and while that's true in some ways, in others, we've experienced some of the same hurts and betrayals. We've gotten through them because we both have supportive families but we're guarded when it comes to relationships, when it comes to *trusting*. And we both guard our passions aka our careers, or in my case, volunteering, with everything we have. Because they're our true lifelines.

He smiles and I return it, our eyes holding. A silent understanding passes between us.

"Your entrees are served," the server announces.

I sit back in my seat, averting my gaze as embarrassment floods my cheeks. Theo chuckles, the sound rumbly. We thank our server, and our eyes connect again.

"If you ever want to talk about anything," Theo offers tentatively, "you can always confide in me, Sofia. No matter what."

"You too," I agree.

"Then let's eat."

I dip my head and cut into my steak, closing my eyes as I chew my first bite. Because it's delicious. This entire night is so much more than I anticipated.

While Theo and I started out as a carefree hookup on a beach, he's quickly becoming much more than that. Much more than any other relationship I've experienced in the past.

More than I even knew existed.

CHAPTER 13
THEO

"Are you ready for the season opener?" Sofia asks me over dessert.

"I hope so," I say slowly. "I've been working out hard all summer."

Her gaze zeroes in on my bicep and she smirks. "It shows."

I snort, flexing for her because…damn, old habits die hard. Sobering, I give her the truth. "I'm not sure how much you know about last season…"

"I read how it all unfolded in that gossip magazine in Maui," she admits, pink tinging her cheeks. I don't know why she's embarrassed. It's common nature for someone to dig for info about a person they just slept with.

"If anyone should be embarrassed, it's me. I messed things up big time for the play-offs. I'm surprised Coach even started me this season. But back when Easton Scotch was in rehab, I filled in for his position for a while. I can play both sides of the ice, switch from left wing to right wing, and I guess Coach was giving me a shot based on my previous performance and not how much trouble I caused last season."

"So this is your chance to prove yourself."

"Exactly. This time, I can't mess it up. I can't be the source of more disharmony on the team which is why," I pause and shift closer to Sofia, "Sofia, I think we should tell Jesse about us."

She inhales a sharp breath, her eyes narrowing. "About Maui?"

"About now. Whatever this is"—I gesture between us—"trust me when I tell you it's real. I can't lie to your brother, my teammate, about having feelings for his sister. But I won't say anything if you're not feeling this. We'll just go our separate ways and be…I don't know, friends."

"Friends?" She arches an eyebrow. "You know that's highly unlikely. It'd be too…hard."

"I definitely feel more than friendship for you."

"Me too," she admits. "Let me talk to my brother."

I hesitate. "I don't want him to think I pulled one over on him."

"He won't," she assures me. "I know how to tell him, what to say. And afterwards, you can come by. Bring a pizza or something, and we'll hang out. The three of us."

"Really?" Some of the tension in my shoulders eases at the hope in her expression. I was hesitant to bring this up to her, worried she would shoot me down. I never expected her to agree so easily. Or quickly.

She reaches across the table and intertwines her hand with mine. "Really, Theo. I want to…try this with you."

"Good. Ready to get out of here?"

"If you're taking me back to your place, then I've been ready since the second I saw you tonight. You rock that leather jacket well for a trust-fund kid."

I laugh. "You pegged me, Sof."

I signal for the check, settle the bill, and Sofia and I make our way to the parking lot. I can't get her back to my condo fast enough. But I also don't want to rush her. I don't want to do anything that will make her second-guess the chance she's giving me.

"Sofia," I say when we're back in my condo, her coat slung over the back of my couch, heels on the floor.

She looks up, her face unreadable. While her eyes are heated, her mouth is firm, as if she's waiting for me to disappoint her. And dammit, that's the last thing I want to do. That's why I want to be completely honest with her before this goes any further.

"I have a past," I blurt out.

Her lips soften the slightest bit. "So do I."

"Yeah," I agree, tilting my head. "But mine is in the press. All over the media. I did a lot of dumb shit. I hurt a lot of people."

She frowns.

"My parents were worried about me. Preston kept throwing around the names of rehab centers. My teammate, my friend, Declan Yaeger wasn't there for his wife because I got him mixed up in my mess. I let my team down. I've been with women, a lot of them, whose names I didn't know. Whose names I didn't care to find out. I've been reckless as hell. I've been called every damn name in the book and most of the time, I deserved it. I know what my reputation is; I know what my past looks like. But baby, I want you to know, before this goes any further, that I'm not that guy anymore." My arms spread out to my sides, palms up, as if I could show her I mean what I say. And I can; over time, I can prove my worth to Sofia. But tonight, I don't want lies between us. I want her to know exactly what she's getting into, the fuckups Eddie Sims made last season, and the man I'm trying to grow back into. Theo.

She rolls her lips together, her expression thoughtful. "What changed?"

I huff out a laugh. I like that she calls me on my shit, digs deeper and demands answers. "You're good for me, Sof."

"Maybe. But I need to make sure you're good for me. Not just for tonight but…"

"But for all of it."

"Yeah," she agrees softly. She sits on the couch, and I sit on the other end, tossing the stupid throw pillows my mom ordered on the floor. How many of these damn things do you need anyway? "So what changed?"

"I did," I say slowly. "Last season, that article you read in the magazine, that was the wake-up call I needed. It's so fucking cliché, but when Delphine and I broke up, I did all the stupid shit that guys who are hurting do. I was killing it on the ice, the total stereotype of a big-man-on-campus complex. Women were everywhere now that I was single. I went out, I got drunk, I hooked up. Repeated it the following weekend. And then, I got recruited by the Hawks. When I first started playing, because Easton was out, it was like my college experience on steroids."

"You were in high demand?" she says it like a joke, but I see the wariness in her eyes.

"It's embarrassing how much I leaned into hockey as my identity. It provided a free pass to act like a dick half the time, to get into stupid trouble, to not answer for my actions. And because I went by Eddie Sims, the blowback didn't land on my family, which was a bonus. I think Mom knew the shit I was doing because she tried to get me to come home more. She and Dad started traveling to attend my games, but I was careful not to mention them to the team, not to expose their identifies. Because then I wouldn't just be party guy Eddie, I'd be Theodore Edward Lawrence, heir to a fucking conglomerate. A legacy."

"I get that. You wanted to have your fun without hurting your family."

"Yeah, but I had too much fun. Got too cocky. Let hockey be my excuse for the way I acted, as if playing hockey meant you didn't have to be caring or compassionate or a fucking human with women. And then that night, we were in the play-offs against the Knights, and I went out in LA. Like an idiot, I got wasted out of my mind, and there was a drug bust. Yaeger tried to pull me from the club but ended up getting arrested along with me. And I was pissed at him. He was furious, spouting off at me, and I remember looking at him, thinking what the hell happened to you, man? You used to be fun and now you're a fucking boring husband who can't hang? The next day, we were released. Yaeger's agent, Callie, and Austin picked us up, and Yaeger's frantic, trying to get in touch with Vivi. He learns, in the fucking car coming back from jail, that she might be miscarrying their baby. He didn't even know she was pregnant. And he's calling hospitals, trying to get in touch with her."

Sofia's face is pale, bleached of color, her eyes fearful. "And you got it?"

"I got it. I was looking at him thinking, this is the kind of guy you were supposed to grow into. Instead, you fucking cost him a moment, an important one with his wife. He didn't even know he was gonna be a daddy. I bet if he wasn't at Lantern, dealing with my shit, he would have known. Then we had to play the game, Scotch went down, I got called up and I"—I bite my lip—"shit the bed, let the team down."

Understanding lines Sofia's face. She reaches for me, her hand curling around my knee. "But you learned from it."

"It was still too late," I whisper, letting her see the agony I feel every time I think back to last season. "It wasn't only the game, which was awful. It was Yaeger. And Vivi. I made a bad situation a million times worse for one of the guys I admire most."

"But you admitted it. You fessed up to it. The only thing you can do now is try harder, be better, move forward."

"Yeah," I agree, taking her hand in mine and pressing our palms together. Our fingers lace naturally, like we've been holding hands for years. "That's what I want you to know.

This whole summer, I kept my head down. I went home to California, stayed with my parents, and coached an awesome group of kids. I worked out constantly, played tennis with Dad, fucking scrapbooked with Mom. Helped Heather with wedding plans and menu tastings when Preston was working. Played video games with my brother. I fell off the map to get my head right and then, I met you. The night we met, it was real for me. It was so much more intense than anything I've had in years, I was scared I'd fuck it up. And I did."

"That wasn't all your fault. I got spooked when I read the article."

"But you should have." I squeeze her hand. "I never showed you that you could trust me. That night, we barely knew each other. I told you you picked the wrong Lawrence and it's true. There's no man as good as my brother. But I swear, Sof, I'm trying to do better. And I want you, baby. I'm all in."

"The fact that you care this much means something, Theo. Now you need to let me decide the rest." She smiles warmly, her eyes back to liquid chocolate.

"And what do you decide?" I murmur, liking the spark in her gaze.

"It's time for you to kiss me, Lawrence." She scrunches her nose and I laugh.

"Happy to, Carpenter." I lean forward and touch my lips to hers.

I feel her mouth curve into a smile under mine, and I smile back before the two of us laugh. We pull back slightly, staring into each other's eyes with a lightness that didn't exist before.

It's different now that I've come clean. She's confided in me from the get-go and now, I've been honest with her. She knows about my family, she knows about my past, she knows about all the stupid shit I got caught up in. She knows and she still wants this with me. Tomorrow, we tell her brother and then…for the first time in years, I'll have a girlfriend. A woman I want to carve out a future with.

I lean forward again. Sofia's breath hitches as our playfulness turns more soulful. This time, I kiss her harder and her hands come to the sides of my face, sliding back into my hair. She tugs lightly and I deepen our kiss, shifting my body over hers.

Sofia lays down on the couch, pulling my body closer. "Make me feel something real, Theo."

"I'm gonna make you feel everything, baby," I promise her. And I mean it. Mind, body, and soul, I want to light Sofia up like the sunshine she is.

CHAPTER 14
SOFIA

I fall into Theo's kiss as easily as I did in Maui. The chemistry between us is effortless, undeniable. I want him because he makes me feel everything. Desired and cherished. Valued and wanted.

My legs twine around his hips and he sinks in between my thighs, his hard length pressing against my core. I jump from the contact, but he doesn't chuckle. He kisses me harder, his body shadowing mine. Theo's hand comes to the side of my face as he pulls back. He lifts my chin and stares into my eyes. "You're changing the game for me, Sof. And this, with you, it changes everything. You know that right?"

"Yes."

"You're not going to ghost me tomorrow?" he asks playfully, but I note the zip of fear in his eyes, and my heart cracks. Because Theo's laid himself bare. He's split himself wide open and shared all the dark things he keeps buried. His name, his family, his mistakes and failures. He gave them to me for safe keeping. For the first time, I realize how much my skipping out on him, not being his date to his brother's wedding when he doesn't introduce women to his family, must have hurt. I was so caught up in my own feelings of betrayal that I never realized I hurt him. Sure, he seems untouchable but under his hard exterior, Theo is like the rest of us. A mere mortal with insecurities and hang-ups. The realization makes me want him more.

"I'm not going anywhere, Theo. I like you again, remember?" I joke, but he correctly reads the seriousness underlining my words.

He nods once, his thumb brushing over my cheekbone. Then, he buries his hand in my hair, drops his face to mine, and kisses me like he'll never get enough. Like every second counts.

And it does. I close my eyes and revel in the moment, soaking up each touch and taste. The brush of his fingertips against my skin as they slip up my skirt. The softness of his mouth as it flutters over my navel and the wetness of his tongue as it dips inside. I memorize the melding of blue and green in his gaze. The appreciation in his eyes causes my heart to race and anticipation to tighten my body.

Theo leans back to undo the row of buttons on his shirt, but I swat his hands away. I lean up, his thighs gripping mine, and pop the buttons open. It shouldn't be erotic, but it is. Because when I look up and Theo's eyes find mine, I imagine doing this for him after an away game. Seeing him for the first time in days and having lived through the intensity of missing him. I can picture us married, in our own condo, decorated with photos of us and our journey. I can see it all in a blink and instead of feeling scared, I want to fall into this fantasy and stay there. Live there until it develops into reality.

"What are you thinking about?" Theo whispers, his hands capturing mine as the last button falls open and his shirt parts down the center.

"You and me," I admit, meeting his eyes.

He grins, kissing me once. "Don't ever stop, okay?"

"Never," I promise.

I push his shirt off his shoulders, undo the button on his jeans, and flop back to enjoy every sensation that Theo pulls from my body. Every thought he inspires in my mind. And the rush of love already swelling in my heart.

Theo Lawrence makes me feel everything imaginable on the couch in his living room. I gasp when he rolls on a condom and slides into me. He stills, his eyes meeting mine.

"Go slow," I murmur.

He nods, pulling back slightly before inching in a little more. Slowly, he works up a pace that has me shattering and him hollering out my name.

When he pulls out, a sheen of blood coats the condom and I blush hard, completely mortified.

Theo tips his head at me. "You know what this means?"

"What?" I whisper, too embarrassed to meet his gaze.

He lifts my chin and winks. "It's time for a shower."

I snort, my relief mixing with his humor. Theo leads me to the shower and even though he tries to hold back, murmuring that he doesn't want to hurt me, and I must be sore, I'm too caught up for us to stop.

And then, the following morning, again.

JESSE LOOKS up when I enter the condo.

"Hey." He stands from the couch and shakes his phone at me. "I was starting to get worried. Where've you been?"

I clear my throat, embarrassed to be caught by my brother. Not that he thinks I'm a saint or anything, but I should have given him a heads-up that I wasn't coming home last night. "I didn't think you'd be home this early."

He narrows his eyes. "You still could have messaged. And I just walked in."

I drop my purse and coat on the couch and walk to the kitchen. I need coffee. Mainly because Theo worked me over but I'm not going to admit that to Jesse.

Relieved to see the coffee pot is already full, I pour two mugs, adding a splash of milk to each. When I turn, Jesse is standing right there and I gasp, my hand shaking. Some of the coffee spills on the floor.

"Shit," I mutter, placing down the mugs.

"I got it." My brother springs into action, quickly cleaning up the mess. He presses one of the mugs in my hand and places his hand in the center of my back, guiding me to the kitchen table.

"What's wrong?" I sit down, giving him a long look to understand his behavior.

He takes a gulp of his coffee, hissing as it burns his tongue. "That's what I'm about to ask you."

I frown. "What do you mean?"

Jesse shakes his head. "Staying out all night? Not calling? I thought you outgrew this shit."

I open my mouth to defend myself, but he continues.

"I know your annual tests are coming up…"

My heart sinks as I understand his meaning. This is the thundercloud. It never lets up, never eases. Even now, years in remission, and my brother automatically links my staying out all night to a relapse. To my need to take in as much as possible in the shortest amount of time, in case that time stops existing. I take his hand and squeeze. His eyes drop to our joined fingers and fear skates over his expression. "It's not that. It's not what you're thinking."

He looks up tentatively. "Then what's going on, Sofia?"

"I met someone," I blurt out.

For a blink, Jesse's expression clears, his worries from a moment ago dissipating. But then he switches into big brother mode, and his eyes narrow. "Who? When? Is that where you were all night?"

I nod, rolling my lips together. Should I tell him about Maui? Does that make it better or worse? Deciding to be as truthful as possible while skating over the more unpleasant details, I say, "It's one of your teammates. Th-Eddie."

Jesse's eyebrows snap together as understanding dawns. "Sims took you out all night and didn't have the decency to—"

"I met him in Maui," I cut him off before Theo's fear is realized and Jesse thinks my brother went behind his back. I don't know how, since I'm clearly a person who can make my own decisions, but dating big brother's teammates never bodes well at the start.

"What?" Jesse asks.

"I didn't know he would be your teammate. Hell, I didn't even know he was a hockey player. But I met him, Theo—"

"Eddie."

I clear my throat. "Eddie—"

"Why'd you call him Theo?" Jesse demands. "Did he give you the wrong fucking name or some shit?"

I sigh. This isn't going as I hoped. "No. His full name is Theodore Edward Lawrence. His mom's maiden name is Sims. His family calls him Theo and since I met him while he was on vacation with his family, attending his brother's wedding, I knew him as Theo."

My brother regards me coolly, his eyes narrowed. But he doesn't interrupt so I forge ahead.

"It was after Don."

Jesse winces, reading between the lines.

"And I, well, I really like him."

"*Theo.*"

I snort, the irony of this situation not lost on me. If only Theo could stick to one name. "I like him a lot, Jesse. He wanted to tell you about us—"

"Us?"

I grip his wrist. "He wanted to be honest from the start, but I wanted to have a real first date first so…"

"So last night was your first date and you didn't come home until this morning?" Jesse pulls his wrist away and folds his arms over his chest.

"Well, yes," I say truthfully. "But Theo is different—"

Jesse rolls his eyes.

"You know he's different," I say more forcefully. "And I invited him over later so we could all hang out. It's important to him that you guys are on the same page. Trust me, if anyone wanted to keep this quiet for longer, it was me. I'm asking you to please give him, me and him, a chance."

"You're serious about this? Him?" Jesse asks after a moment.

"Yes," I say clearly, staring right at him.

"This isn't another—"

"No," I cut him off. "This isn't some whirlwind that I'm caught up in."

Jesse regards me, and I know he's recalling all the times I said something similar. All the decisions I swore were right without giving them the consideration they deserved. The whims I embraced because why not? But this is different; I *feel* differently about Theo.

Jesse blows out a deep breath. "You know no one likes to see their little sister date their teammate, right?"

"I know."

"But since you just had your first date, I can't exactly knock Sims for wanting to be straight."

"No, you can't."

"So, yeah, whatever. We'll do pizza. I'll give…this…a chance. But, Sofia, you've gotta be upfront with me. I've got a lot going on right now and your past few months have been intense. You broke up with Don, moved to Boston, are re-enrolling in school, and got tests coming up. I'm worried about you."

"You always worry about me," I remind him, sticking out my tongue.

He snorts and shakes his head. "Can you blame me?"

"No," I say. "I like that you care so much."

"Always, Sofia. You need anything, I'm here. Just make sure you're not rushing this thing with Sims. If it's for real, take your time. There's no need to be impulsive."

"I'm not—" I cut myself off, because Jesse is offering his opinion. I need to hear him out. "Okay."

"Okay." He stands from the table. "I'm going to crash."

"Date keep you busy all night?"

"Not going there with you, little sister. Call me when the pizza's ready."

I laugh. "Yeah, okay."

Jesse's bedroom door closes behind him. I force myself to stand, intent on taking a shower, followed by a nap. When I undress, the blood in my underwear catches my eye and I frown. What the hell? Yeah, Theo and I got caught up in the moment and it was intense, but I wouldn't describe it as rough.

Shaking my head, I take a quick shower. Then, I dress and crawl into bed.

My phone buzzes with an incoming FaceTime and I smile.

"Hey, Dad," I answer.

Dad's face comes into view, his smile wide when he sees me. "Sofie girl. How you doing?" His eyes narrow as he takes in my headboard. "You not feeling well?"

I chuckle. "More like sleeping off a hangover."

I know the info shouldn't make my dad laugh but it's clear that he's relieved I feel fine, okay enough to get drunk and sleep it off.

"Good night, then?" he asks.

"One of the best." I yawn, my eyes heavy.

"Ah." Understanding ripples over his expression. "You met someone?"

"I did."

"And you're not going to share all the details with your father?"

I laugh, shaking my head. "Eventually. But right now, Daddy, I'm sorry, I'm—"

"Exhausted."

I nod.

"Go to sleep, Sofia. But call me this week; I want to hear about your life in Boston."

"Promise," I swear. "Love you."

"Love you more," Dad replies.

I flash him a smile before disconnecting, ready to fall asleep. But an email comes in and the alert distracts me.

As soon as I open the email, my chest twists. It's from my doctor in Michigan, letting me know that he's transferred my care to Mass General. I have an appointment in two weeks.

My stomach sinks at the email, at the meaning behind it. Jesse was right, my annual tests are coming up. Each year, a sense of dread dulls my mind and spirit for the days leading up to and following the tests.

The thundercloud is firmly in place, hovering overhead, ready to burst.

CHAPTER 15
THEO

"Hey, man." Jesse pulls open the door. He greets me with the same easy smile, but his eyes aren't as warm. In fact, he looks more menacing than I expected.

"What's going on?" I hold out my fist and he bumps it.

"Sofia just ran out to grab some drinks." He turns and I follow him inside the condo, placing the pizza boxes on the kitchen table. "You and my sister, huh?"

Okay, so he's going right in. "I want to be straight with you."

He hops up onto the kitchen counter and tosses a bottle of water at me. "Let's hear it."

"I know what my reputation is," I start.

"It's not good."

"It's not who I am."

"Now or ever?" He tilts his head.

"Now," I admit, going for honesty. "Look, man, I was a mess last season. But this summer, I got my head on straight. I went home, spent time with my family, coached. And then, I met Sofia."

"In Maui."

"At my brother's wedding."

Jesse sighs. "Look, I just want what's best for my sister. And she's really into you and that's all good but man, my sister loves too hard, if you know what I mean?"

I shrug, waiting for him to continue.

"She's impulsive, spontaneous. Everything for her is about a moment, having a meaningful experience. Or connection. I adore Sofia, and God knows she hasn't had it easy. Beating childhood cancer the way she did, dealing with the blowback—"

"What do you mean by that? What way?" I interrupt.

Jesse swears and crosses his arms over his chest. "She had a hard go of things. For a long time, it seemed like she wouldn't make it to the next day. When she got better, in a lot of ways, it was a goddamn miracle. And man, my sister did not take that lightly. She threw herself into living, into wanting to feel every high and every low, each sunrise and sunset, all of it. More than anything, she wants this great big love. And I'm not trying to blow up her spot by telling you all these things about her, I just want you to understand who Sofia is. Trust me, you've never met another girl like her."

"I know that. And I know who she is." I temper my growl, not liking that Jesse's insinuating his sister is some type of handful that I can't handle.

Jesse shakes his head. "You're hearing me all wrong."

"Then say what you're trying to say."

He kicks the heel of his sneaker against the cabinet. "I'm saying Sofia has big feelings and she loves hard. If you're not able to see that, to know that she's already all in with you, and be all in with her, then I'm asking you to let her go. Because if you break my sister's heart, you and I will have a problem, and I don't want that shit for the team."

I stand straighter, impressed that Jesse just threw down like that for Sofia. "You're a rookie," I remind him.

"I don't care about anything as much as I care about my sister."

I smile.

"What?"

"Good. I'm glad she has you in her corner. But Jesse, she's got me too. I'm all in and I like that she's got big feelings and a huge heart. I like that she's enamored with the mundane things of life. Being with her…it's like an awakening."

"Yeah," Jesse agrees. "All right then." He slides off the countertop and holds out a hand. "Treat her right."

"Always." I shake his hand.

"And what the fuck am I supposed to call you?"

I laugh, shaking my head. "I'm going to talk to the team but…you can call me Theo."

Jesse cracks a smile, as if that admission let him know I'm serious about Sofia. "Good to meet you, Theo."

"You too, man."

"I'm back!" The front door opens, and Sofia's voice rings out.

Her brother and I turn, and when she sees the two of us together, the biggest smile stretches across her face. "You guys! See, I told you this would be great." She places a plastic bag with cans of soda down on the table, next to the two pizzas I left there. Then she walks toward us and flings her arms around Jesse and me in an attempt at a hug.

Jesse rolls his eyes and I snort, patting her back lightly. But Sofia just keeps on squeezing us, happy for the three of us to eat pizza together. Like it's some kind of victory and not a random weeknight in September.

When she pulls back she grins up at me, her eyes warm. "You hungry?"

"Starving," I reply, getting lost in her gaze.

"Disgusting," Jesse remarks, stepping out of our little huddle to grab some pizza. "I'm picking the movie."

Sofia laughs and I kiss her hello, recognizing how some of these tiny moments, the ones that seem insignificant, are extraordinary.

AFTER JESSE and I got on the same page, I realized it's time for me to come clean with my team. Now that my personal and professional lives are melding, I need to tell the guys on the team the truth. The last thing I want is to start this season with more bullshit between us. Not when I swore to myself that I was going to do better. Part of that entails honesty and I've been dodging it for too long.

"What's going on, man?" Yaeger asks as he slides into the seat across from mine. His tone is conversational, but his eyes are watchful, as if expecting bad news.

"Can't we just grab lunch?" I play it off.

"With Easton and Cap too? Nah, something's up." Yaeger lifts an eyebrow. "You in trouble?"

My chest squeezes at the insinuation but I can't fault him for it. For too long, the answer would have been yes. Too many times, I've gotten myself in trouble and the fallout landed on the shoulders of my team.

"No," I reply, noting the relief in Yaeger's eyes. "I...I just want to share some things with you guys."

"Okay," Yaeger agrees, leaning back in his chair and picking up the menu.

"How's Vivi feeling?"

Yaeger looks up from the menu. His expression changes as he grins. "She's so good, Sims. We're not finding out the sex of the baby but man...I think it's a girl."

"That's awesome, Yaeger. I'm happy for you guys." I mean it, too. In fact, as I chat with Yaeger about Vivi's last prenatal appointment, I can't help but wonder what it would be like if I was going to be a father. The pride, the excitement, the miracle of it all... Yaeger wears it well. I hope one day, I get that chance.

Easton and Austin arrive a few minutes later and after a quick glance that things seem cool, they sit down. We order a round of beers, Easton opting for a Coke, and some sushi nachos and chips and guac to start.

"Love this place," Austin declares, biting into a chip.

"Gotta thank Torsten for making it our spot," East agrees, referencing one of the Hawks former players, Torsten Hansen. He retired two seasons ago and now splits his time between New York and Norway with his wife, but he was a big foodie and a lot of the team's favorite restaurants are thanks to his pulse on the food and beverage scene.

"What's going on?" Austin asks me.

"First," East interrupts, pointing at me. "I want you to know that Sofia Carpenter is one of the greatest things that's happened to the Hawks in a long time. If things go south with you, I'll probably take her side."

"What?" I sputter.

Yaeger looks confused but Austin lets out a laugh.

"She signed the girls up for pole dancing, man," Easton explains, tossing a hand in the air. His eyes dance as he chuckles. "Fucking pole dancing. I can't wait for Claire to start and come home to me. Might install a fucking pole in my bedroom."

Yaeger snickers. "Damn. I don't know whether to be relieved or depressed that Vivi's pregnant."

"I'm sure Sofia will rope her in after delivery," I say, laughing with the guys. She mentioned her pole-dancing class to me, but I didn't know she got the BHH girls in on it. I love that she's bonding with them. I love that she's getting everyone to do something new and outside their comfort zone.

"She's the best." East points at me. "So this better not be to tell us that you ran her off."

"Nah, it's not that, man." I shake my head.

The table goes quiet, and I know this is it. The moment

when I fully embrace my identity as Theo Lawrence, son of Lance and Margaret, heir to an American dynasty.

"Is everything okay?" Easton asks after a beat, his tone devoid of judgment. That's one of the things I like best about East, he doesn't judge or hold a grudge.

"Yep. I just, look, I want to be completely upfront with you all, with the team, before the season starts. Last season ended on a really shitty note and that's on me—"

"You've already made amends for that," Easton reminds me. It's true, I did my round of apologies with the team in the weeks that followed the big loss, but it still doesn't feel like enough. I don't know if it ever will.

"I swore to myself I'd do better this year, be more. All in, straight up, nothing shady," I say.

Yaeger, Austin, and Easton stare at me, waiting for the news.

"I don't talk about my family a lot," I sputter, trying to decide the best way to start this confession that I should have owned years ago, back when I first started gelling with the team, back when I realized how much the guys had my back. Instead, I kept everyone at arm's length and leaned into the party guy persona that was easy to pull off. "Back when I got called up, my parents' businesses, their reputation was recovering from a major hit. I didn't want my name linked to them, always drudging up shit from the past, and I didn't want my career to be shadowed by their reputation."

"Who are your parents?" Austin asks, cutting to the chase.

"Lance and Margaret Lawrence."

Yaeger sucks in a breath, Austin's eyes widen, and East looks at me blankly.

"Who are they?" Easton asks for clarification.

"Like the Bill and Melinda Gates of healthcare," Yaeger explains.

I narrow my eyes. "How'd you know that?"

"Seriously? My wife runs a foundation," he replies.

Oh yeah, I forgot about that.

"How'd you fly under the radar for so long?" Yaeger asks.

"Professionally, I use my middle name, Edward, Eddie, and my mom's maiden name, Sims, to create distance," I announce. "I have been for years."

"Eddie's not your real name?" Easton's mouth drops open.

"It's Theodore. Theo," I come clean.

"No shit?" East asks, still surprised.

"It's like we don't even fucking know you," Yaeger rattles off, his eyes narrowed. Since he's one of my closest friends on the team, I expected his frustration, but I hate that he's hurt by my confession. How many of the guys will feel blindsided by this? Will it affect the team's harmony?

"Yeah, you do. You guys know me. I was just trying to protect my family, that's all. But you guys are also my family, and I don't want to start this season without you knowing the truth. I'm sorry if you feel caught off guard or like I wasn't open, but I'm trying to be better about that," I say.

Yaeger keeps glaring at me. Slowly, understanding dawns. "Shit, man, this is about Sofia, isn't it?"

Austin groans. "You said you were going to fix that."

"I did." I grin. "I talked to Jesse, and he knows what's up. I met Sofia in Maui."

"Maui?" Easton repeats. "When the hell were you in Maui?"

"Over the summer. My brother got married there and my family rented a bunch of villas. We—"

"Rented villas?" East repeats. "No way, man. I'm with Yaeger. We don't fucking know you. Because if we knew that you could have rented a villa in Maui, we wouldn't have been picking up your bar tab all these years."

The guys crack up and I grin.

For years, I didn't want anyone to know who my family is because people always tried to take advantage, score an invite to something, get an introduction. But at the ribbing that naturally unfolds, I realize I never had to worry about that with these guys. Not with the Hawks.

"Lunch is on me," I offer.

Easton nods while Austin chuckles.

Yeager regards me for a long moment. "It's Sofia, isn't it?" he asks again.

"Yeah, man. It's Sofia."

Yaeger grins. "I told you when it happened to you, the world would flip."

"It has," I agree. "She makes me want to be better."

Yaeger nods. "And you will be. Because the thought of letting her down—"

"Fucking guts you," East finishes.

Our server, Shell, drops off our lunch entrees.

"Welcome to the club, Sims." Austin holds up his beer. "I'm expecting big things from you this season."

"Thanks, Cap." I clink my glass against his.

"You're off to an okay start, Eddie." East shoots me a grin.

"Thanks, but you can call me Theo," I offer.

Easton nods.

I take a swig of my beer and relax. Things are clicking back into place; they almost seem too good to be true. But I've worked hard to get to this place with the team again. To be honest with myself. To meld my professional and personal lives. It feels good, to have them all lining up.

When I finish lunch with the guys, I call my parents and invite them to our season opener against Atlanta. It's a home game and I'm finally ready to introduce them to a woman I'm seeing, dating, falling for.

I want them to meet Sofia.

CHAPTER 16
SOFIA

"What's the first thing you want to eat?" I ask Sam, leaning back in my chair.

He thinks it over and takes a sip of his coffee. "A steak. With thick cut steak fries. And with Katie, of course."

"Mm, solid choice. How is Kate?"

His eyes crinkle when he smiles. "Can't wait to see my Katie. She sent me a letter this week." He carefully removes a folded-up piece of paper from his pocket. His fingers tremble as he smooths the paper and my throat constricts, remembering how much older my father looked, acted, seemed when he left lockup after only five years.

While I wrote to him frequently, he lived too far away for visits. Plus, he never put me on his approved visitor list, preferring that I not see him in a prison cafeteria-style visiting room.

"She invited me to stay with her and Matt." He taps his index finger against the paper. His eyes shine with emotion when they meet mine. "Can you believe that? She and her husband invited me to live with them while I get on my feet." Sam's mouth twists into a sad smile. "How lucky am I, Sofia?"

"Pretty damn lucky, Sam," I agree, knowing how many inmates don't have a loving, supportive environment to return to.

"Yeah," his tone is rumbly, and he clears his throat. "How's your old man?"

I shrug. "Okay."

"Okay," Sam mimics my tone and I grin. "Come on, Sofia, what's going on? You've been here almost a month. He's not that far away."

"I know. I just, well, I don't want to intrude."

"On him?" Sam's eyebrows nearly fly off his face.

I snicker. "I'm overthinking it, huh?"

"You are. Trust me when I tell you, there's no one in the world your father would rather see than you."

"Yeah…" A year ago, I would have agreed. But since Don and Maui, I'm not so sure. When Dad learned the reason behind my called-off engagement, he retreated into himself. I think he felt bad, guilty, for Don's and my failed relationship. But now, now I'm with Theo and I've never been happier. "I'll call him today."

"You do that, girl."

"I will." I tap Sam's booklet. "Okay, enough chitchat. You've got three questions left. Let's make sure you have your GED before you get out of here."

Sam grins again. "That'll make Katie proud."

"Don't I know it," I agree, pointing at the exercise booklet.

As Sam goes back to solving the equation, my mind wanders to Dad. Is he lonely? Why hasn't he been as forthcoming as usual? Is it because my tests are coming up? Sure, we've been talking, but not like we normally do. Now, there's a wall between us. Doesn't he miss me, want to be part of my life, the same way Kate misses Sam?

THE WEATHER HAS TURNED, and I pull my coat tighter around my shoulders as I leave the prison. I slip behind the wheel of Jesse's SUV and stare at the barbed wire, the prison guards.

Saying goodbye to Sam is difficult and I imagine how heartbreaking it would have been to leave Dad behind. I flip on the ignition and turn up the heat as I think about Dad, the sacrifices he made, the life I cost him.

Is guilt holding me back? Do I not push him for more, more time, more answers, more of himself, because he already paid the ultimate price? He sacrificed his freedom for my life.

After five minutes, I work up the courage to call him. It's my third call this week and relief floods through me when he finally picks up.

"Sofia," his tone is warm.

"Daddy. I've been trying you all week. You okay?"

"Yeah," he laughs. "I went on a fishing trip."

"Oh," I breathe out.

"You don't have to worry about me, Sofia. That's my job."

I press my lips together, my eyes closing as I lean my head back against the headrest. Even now, my dad's always looking out. "Did you catch any fish?"

He laughs, the sound easygoing. "Some, yeah. How are you? How's Boston? That boyfriend?"

"Good. I was hoping now that we're closer, I could come for a visit."

"Anytime. I'd love to see you."

"Or you could come here?" I ask tentatively.

Dad sighs and a few beats of silence tick by. "Sofia, I'd like to come see you. Meet Jesse in person. But…"

"But?"

"I haven't been in a big city in a long time."

"Okay," I say quickly, not wanting him to feel uncomfortable. "I'll come to you."

"That sounds good. I can't wait to hear about your life. All the great things you're doing. How's school?"

"Um…" I clear my throat. "I think I'm starting back up in January." I toss it out on a whim but…am I?

"Nursing, right?"

"Maybe criminal justice?"

Dad sighs and my stomach tightens. "Sofia, you don't have to—"

"I want to."

"Honey, I don't want you to change your passions because of my choices."

"I'm not."

"I want you to have a fulfilling, rewarding, happy life. With a career you adore, a husband, a family that makes you happy. You don't have to take up a cause just because—"

"I have a new boyfriend," I remind him.

Dad's silent for a long moment. "Another pretty boy?"

I snort. "No. That didn't work out because—"

"Of me," Dad interrupts again. Ever since he went to prison, he's retreated from my life. While he's always being there for me, he started keeping his distance on the day-to-day things, as if waiting for the time when I would be embarrassed by him. That day has never come, and I don't know what else I can do to prove to him that it never will.

"Because Don's a douchebag," I clarify. "I love you, Daddy. Nothing bad in my life is because of you, ever."

"I don't know about that, honey. But the new guy. What's his name? What's he do?"

"His name is Theo Lawrence. He's a hockey player. Actually, he's on the same team as Jesse, the Boston Hawks. And he'd love to meet you too. He's nothing like Don, so much more genuine and giving with his time. I think you'd really like him."

A long moment passes. So long that I clear my throat and pull the phone away from ear to make sure we're still connected. "Daddy?"

"I'm here," he says, sounding strangled. "Sorry, honey, I'm getting a call. There's something I need to do. Can I call you back?"

"Um, sure," I respond, confused.

Dad hangs up before I can say anything else. I pull the cell phone away from my ear and stare at it again. We were on the phone for less than seven minutes. Is that all he can give me these days? Did my mention of Theo cause him to hurry off the phone or was it something else? Did he really have another call or commitment to take care of?

I sigh and tap my head against the headrest. I don't feel any better than I did when I left the jail. Why does it feel like every time I make progress with Dad, he pulls back again? What am I missing?

My phone buzzes with an alert and I swear when I read the reminder.

My appointment with the oncologist at Mass General is in three days.

Now, I feel even worse.

"HEY, SOF," Theo greets me, dropping down to kiss my cheek.

I blink up at him and glance around his condo. I must have fallen asleep while he was at practice. "Hey. I'm sorry; I fell asleep. What time is it?"

He sits down on the edge of the couch and cups my cheek.

His eyes narrow in concern. "Just after 7 p.m. You okay, babe? You look beat."

"I feel exhausted," I admit, shifting. Then, I wince.

"What's wrong?"

"Nothing. I think I pulled a muscle in my back at pole dancing. And I had a weird day. This is probably the emotional toll of it." I lift an arm and let it flop back against my legs, gesturing to my sprawled-out form.

"What happened?"

"I don't know... Just a conversation with Sam. Made me think of my dad. But when I called him, he seemed weird."

"Weird how?"

"Just fine and then, suddenly checked out. He rushed me off the phone."

Theo frowns and tucks a strand of hair behind my ear. "Maybe he just has his own things going on."

"Maybe," I say, but deep down, I don't believe that. Something I said caught Dad off guard. I just don't know what it is, or why. "Plus, I have my annual tests this week. They always throw me for a loop."

"Annual tests?" Theo asks.

I give him a soft smile. "I go every year. Just to make sure I'm still in remission. That my cancer isn't back."

At the C word, Theo pales. His hand drops to my shoulder, and he clutches it. "Baby, why didn't you say anything? Shit, Sof, I had no idea. That would throw anyone off their game."

I shrug. "I don't like talking about it. I don't even like thinking about it."

"I get that. But if you want to talk, I'm here. I'd like to understand more about your past...what you went through."

I squeeze his hand gratefully. "Thanks. One day...but not tonight."

"Okay. Can I come with you? To the appointment?"

The back of my nose burns at the thoughtfulness of his

question. Don never once accompanied me to any of my appointments. Jesse would try but he was usually traveling for hockey. Mom always came but right now, she's in Istanbul or Sharm El Sheikh. "It's a long day."

"I don't mind," Theo answers automatically.

I scrunch my nose. "You have a game that night. Atlanta."

"I'll stay with you for as long as I can." His hand finds my cheek again and he dips forward, until our noses touch. "I want to be here for you, Sof. Let me."

"I don't know how, Theo. The last time I tried..." I trail off.

"Baby, I'm not Don," he nearly growls, pulling back.

"Trust me, I know." I look up at him. "My life isn't a guarantee."

"No one's life is."

I snort. "True. I just..." don't want to hurt you. Don't know how to trust this. Don't know why I feel so off-balance.

I don't voice any of these concerns because I feel too scattered to make sense. Whatever's going on with Dad, coupled with my upcoming tests, has shaken me.

"Sofia, you can talk to me." Theo's brow bends and I can tell he's hurt. I'm already hurting him.

I grasp his wrist tighter and take a deep breath. "I don't think I'm making sense, Theo."

"Try, babe."

"I just feel...scared. Like, something is coming. I can't explain it, but something is...off."

His frown deepens. "Okay," he says slowly. "It's normal to feel worried, apprehensive, right?"

I nod. "But it feels like more than that."

"All the more reason I should come with you. Baby, you don't have to do this alone."

"But then, when you leave—"

"I'm not." He cuts me off. "I'm not going anywhere, Sofia." Theo's eyes burn with so much conviction, I want to fall inside of them and stay there. But someone always leaves. There are no guarantees. Only moments. Minutes. How long will ours last?

"Make me feel something, Theo," I demand, suddenly desperate for a connection. *This* connection. With him.

Understanding dawns fierce on his expression. Theo doesn't ask any more questions but kisses me hard, savagely, as if his lips can prove what his words didn't.

That he's here. That he's staying. That we have a real chance.

And I want to believe him so badly that I fall forward into the possibility he presents, and allow myself to drown in him. In this. In us.

CHAPTER 17
THEO

"Yo, man, what's going on with my sister?" Jesse asks the following day after practice.

I pull my practice jersey over my head and plop down on the bench. "I'm worried about her," I admit, not wanting to go behind her back but... "She's stressing about this appointment. I can tell."

Jesse swears. "It's like this every year. But it's something else... Look, I can read my sister better than most. But I don't know what's going on in her head. She seemed to settle into this, into your relationship, all of it easily and I thought..."

"What?" I narrow my eyes, wanting to know all of Jesse's thoughts if they'll help clarify some of Sofia's fears.

"I thought she was settling down a bit, locking into a routine. I worry when I think she's going to fall off the grid. You get that impression, Eddie?"

"Theo," I correct.

He smirks. "Theo." But then his smirk drops, and his expression grows serious. "She's spontaneous. She truly understands the weight, the value, of a moment and tries her best to be present in the present."

"That's not a bad thing."

"No," he agrees. "It's not. But it's distracting when every moment needs to be *a moment*. When everything needs to have some additional significance to prove to Sofia that she's truly living it. Man, her childhood was shit. It was lonely and painful and filled with fear and uncertainty. But her adulthood, it doesn't have to be like that. She just doesn't know how to enjoy it for what it is, to take the days as they are. She rushes sometimes and then when she tries to pump the breaks, it's a goddamn pileup."

"You think she and I rushed this?" I frown. Did we? I mean, we hooked up the night we met and now, she's pretty much living at my place. Shit, is this a pattern I didn't see? A thing I didn't realize was even a thing?

"I don't know," Jesse offers. "I just know something is going on with Sofia and I don't know how to help her if she doesn't let me, or you, in. Maybe I should call Ted but—"

"Who's Ted?" And if Jesse's thinking of calling him, why haven't I ever heard his name before?

"Her dad. He's really great at helping her clarify her thoughts, process shit."

"Her dad," I repeat, something clicking. "She mentioned talking to him the other day. That he was being weird and rushed her off the phone."

Jesse squints at me, disbelief in his expression. "Ted rushed her off the phone? No way, man. Ted adores Sofia; he'll do any-fucking-thing she needs. He wouldn't...unless, maybe they had words or something?" He pauses, the wheels in his head turning. Reaching out, he bumps his fist against my shoulder. "Thanks, man. I'll talk to her."

"No." I stand from the bench.

Jesse turns and tilts his head at me, more in confusion than anger.

"I want in," I clarify. "Whatever she's dealing with, whatever she needs, I'm all in with her, Jesse."

He stares at me for a long moment before his expression

clears and he nods. "All right. Swing by for dinner. We'll... talk to her."

"I don't want her to feel like we're ganging up on her," I worry, wondering if she'll be angry that Jesse and I are clearly discussing her behind her back.

"We're not, man. She needs to feel supported and that's the direction we'll lean into."

"Okay," I agree. "I'll pick up..."

"Thai," he offers.

I snort. "That for you or her?"

Jesse grins. "I gotta shower. See ya later."

"Yeah." I turn away from Jes and swipe up my phone.

MOM

Can't wait to see the game! Dad and I fly in tomorrow.

PRESTON

Mom is over the moon about this weekend.
Hope Sofia is ready for her.

I can't wait to officially introduce Sofia to my parents, as my girl. I just wish it wasn't right now, when she's dealing with so much.

"THIS FEELS LIKE AN INTERVENTION," Sofia announces when I show up with Thai takeout.

"It's not," Jesse assures her, pouring out water glasses.

I place the takeout bags on the kitchen table and wink at Sofia.

"It kind of is," I clarify.

Instead of the anger I expected, she laughs. "Well, then, I

expect the full experience. First, give me a lot of compliments and remind me how amazing I am at balancing all the things. Then, gently suggest areas for improvement. Follow that by an ice cream sundae and hugs and murmurings of 'we're here if you need to talk.'"

I chuckle while Jesse swears good-naturedly.

"Let's eat first," I suggest, pulling out the takeout containers.

Sofia points the end of her fork at her brother. "He's better at this."

"He's a newbie, still trying to feel you out," Jesse replies.

Sofia smirks and takes her seat. "Thanks." She accepts the plate piled with pad thai. "You guys, I'm really fine. I'm just…I'm worried about my appointment."

"And?" Jesse presses.

"And…my dad's been so weird lately," Sofia shares.

Jesse and I exchange a look.

"Do you have any idea why?" I ask, placing plates down for Jesse and me.

Sofia shakes her head, chewing a mouthful of noodles. "No, but he started after I mentioned you."

"Me?" My palm comes up to rest on my chest.

"Yeah. Strange, right?" Sofia asks.

Jesse clears his throat. "Mentioned Theo, as in 'hey-dad-I've-got-a-new-man-in-my-life' or 'hey-I'm-dating-Theo-Lawrence.'"

Confusion wavers over Sofia's face for a moment. "His name," she says finally. "It was after I said your name that Dad rushed me off the phone. He hasn't taken any of my calls since. Sam thinks—"

"You went back to the prison?" Jesse interrupts.

Sofia sighs. "I needed to talk to Sam."

"You could talk to me," Jesse reminds her. "Or him." He points to me.

I've just been reduced to "him." Rolling my eyes, I interject, "What's your dad's name? Maybe our paths have crossed? Or he knows someone in my family?"

"Unlikely," Jesse murmurs. "Sofia's dad is a mechanic in New Hampshire. Your family drives Bentleys."

Sofia smirks again. "His name is Ted Strauss."

"Strauss?" I frown. "But your last name is Carpenter."

"Yeah." She glances at Jesse. "Jesse's dad, Mitch, adopted me after our parents married."

"Why?" I wonder. It's not like Mitch raised her, or has been in her life since she was a little kid… "I thought your Mom remarried when you were like thirteen."

"Fourteen," she clarifies. "But with Dad in prison…well, changing my surname gave me a fresh start. A clean slate."

"Okay," I say slowly, kind of understanding. But… "Wasn't your dad hurt?"

Jesse shakes his head. "It was Ted's idea. After the childhood Sofia had, he wanted her to have a real shot at starting over."

"Okay," I say again, holding up a hand. I don't want to press. Even if it seems strange to me, Sofia and Jesse obviously have no issue with it. "Well, I can ask my parents if they know a Ted Strauss."

Sofia shrugs. "Or I could be reading way too much into this."

"You're not." Jesse shakes his head. "You know your dad better than anyone in the world. If you think he's being weird, then something's off."

"Yeah," Sofia agrees, taking a gulp of water. "Or it's me? You know how I get before my annuals."

Jesse reaches over and squeezes her hand. "Everything's going to be fine, Sofia."

"And if it's not?" she asks Jesse, but her eyes are trained on mine.

"Then we figure it out together," I remind her.

My reassurance settles her some and she picks up her

fork, digging into her pad thai. But my appetite is gone. The back of my neck prickles with a warning, with a strange reminder. Wisps of a memory, long forgotten but still lurking along the edges of mind, flickers. I know that name. Ted Strauss. But from where? How?

I push some rice around my plate and look at Sofia. She's effortless, beautiful and thoughtful and overflowing with zest for life. For everything. I can't lose her.

Even though I can't shake the feeling that I will. That something, from her past or mine, is about to wreak havoc on the life we're creating. Something that's going to change everything.

"You not hungry?" she asks, her gaze trained on my plate.

"Not as hungry as I thought." I shoot her a smile and scoop up some rice, going through the motions of eating.

But my head is spinning.

Ted Strauss.

Strauss...

How the hell do I know that name? What does it mean?

CHAPTER 18
SOFIA

I f I wasn't so preoccupied at the thought of meeting Theo's parents, I'd think he was starting to get cold feet about officially introducing me. But I'm much too busy getting my hair blown out, my nails done, and making reservations for us to have dinner with his parents.

Lance and Margaret Lawrence descend on Boston the same way they arrived in Maui. In style. The moment I see them, all warm smiles and friendly eyes, I relax. Of course, when I planned Heather and Preston's wedding, they were lovely. But going from the wedding coordinator to their son's girlfriend is an entirely different ballgame. Lance is Theo in twenty-something years. He's got the same blue-green eyes, self-assuredness, and envy-inspiring hair.

But Margaret is a rainbow. I'm anticipating the shrewd eyes and assessing questions Mrs. Servino first greeted me with when she learned I was dating Don. Instead, Margaret wraps me in a hug, right in the foyer of Theo's condo, and murmurs, "I'm just so happy for you and Theo. It's great to see you here, sweetheart."

Her acceptance rolls over me, warming parts I didn't realize were cold. I had steeled myself for her questions, her uncertainties, hell, her downright dismissal. Instead, she tucks my hand into the crook of her elbow and, after I exchange introductions with Mr. Lawrence, whisks me into Theo's kitchen for a coffee and a chat.

Even that's not the grilling I anticipate. Margaret fixes us Nespresso coffees and places our mugs down on the island top. Then she slips onto the barstool next to me. "Tell me about yourself, Sofia. All I know is that you plan the most exquisite weddings, love volunteer work, and have changed my son for the better." She grins. "I want to thank you for all your work on Heather and Preston's wedding. It was gorgeous. Heather was so upset that you had to rush out before the wedding ceremony, but she couldn't stop gushing over what a wonderful job you did, down to every last detail."

I smile at the praise, a twinge of guilt flaring for leaving Maui prior to Heather's walk down the aisle. While I made up an excuse to the bride and groom, as well as the Servinos, Theo knew the truth. The fact that he didn't put me on blast, even after I ghosted him, allows me to relax in my barstool. "Heather and Preston's wedding was my favorite to be part of during my time at Lely Prive," I admit.

"Were you there a long time?"

"About eight months. I'm not sure how much you know about my past, Mrs. Lawrence, but—"

"Please, call me Margaret."

"Margaret." I smile. Mrs. Servino never invited me to call her by her first name, not even after I was engaged to her son. "Well, Don Servino and I were engaged but it didn't work out. We broke up earlier in the summer, but I didn't want to leave before seeing Heather's wedding plans play out so…"

"So you stayed," Margaret murmurs, surprised. "That was very thoughtful of you, Sofia. It must have been difficult to remain at the resort after things didn't work out the way you hoped." She shakes her head, looking genuinely distraught for me.

"Well, it wasn't that bad," I backtrack. "I mean, Maui."

She laughs, the sound genuine. "True." She takes a sip of her coffee.

"And I met your son," I add.

Her smile widens. "At the rehearsal dinner."

"Yes."

"And now you're in Boston too!" She shakes her head again, this time in disbelief.

"It was a surprise for me too. After Maui, I went to my brother's in San Antonio. A few weeks later, Jesse was traded to the Hawks and I jumped at the chance to move with him. I knew I'd cross paths with Theo but…I never expected this." I wave an arm toward the living room where Theo and his dad are having a conversation.

"Well, you know what they say about life."

"What?" I ask.

"It happens while you're busy making plans," Margaret explains.

I nod, thinking that over. "It's true," I say after a moment, catching Margaret off guard. My childhood, my illness, isn't something I usually share the first time I speak with someone but… "Did Theo tell you I was sick? As a child?"

"No," she says slowly, her brow furrowing.

"I had leukemia," I admit. "A rare type that guaranteed a good chunk of my childhood was spent in hospital beds, undergoing tests and treatments."

"I'm so sorry," Margaret murmurs, compassion sweeping her expression.

"I'm only mentioning it because…well, I truly understand what you mean about life happening when you're making plans. That's why, at some point, I stopped making plans and just started living. Being fully invested in the day-to-day without much thought about the future, or even next week."

"I understand that. When you have your certainty and stability taken at such a young age, thinking too far ahead would seem…scary. Maybe even silly."

"Exactly," I agree, enjoying her candor. So many people try to tiptoe around issues that make them uncomfortable. Whether those be about health or politics or religion, I've learned early on that people don't like to be uncomfortable. But how else can you grow without experiencing the discomfort of growing pains? "I know things between Theo and me seem like they happened fast. Maybe too fast. But I want you to know that your son made a big impression on me the night I met him. Reconnecting with Theo in Boston is changing a lot of my mindset. For the first time, I want to look to the future and see more than just today… I tried that with Don and when it fell apart, I thought maybe I wasn't meant to have the future or the family. But with Theo, I want it. And I'm happy you and Mr. Lawrence came this weekend. I want to spend this time with you, Margaret. I hope you don't think me too forward for saying so."

Theo's mom smiles at me warmly. She reaches for my hand and wraps her fingers around mine. "Not at all, Sofia. In fact, I find your honesty refreshing. In my world, too many people say what they think you want to hear, instead of just owning their truth. I think you being straightforward is brave and I admire you for it. And not related, but Lance and I own several hospitals. If there's ever anything we can help with, regarding your health, please reach out. We have a network of resources we can tap into if need be."

"Thank you. That's kind of you. I have my annual tests tomorrow and they always put me on edge."

"I'd imagine so," she agrees. "How are you liking Boston?"

"Very much," I say, surprising myself. But it's true. In just one month, I've fallen a little in love with my life here. Jesse was right; Boston isn't Maui. It's so much better because I'm surrounded by the right people. My brother, Theo, the Hawks girls, Sam. I'm creating a life here that I want to live, for more than a moment, maybe for a lifetime. "I'm enrolling back in school in January. In the meantime, I do a lot of volunteering."

"Yes, Heather told us about your volunteering. Where are you spending your energies here? I know one of Theo's teammate's wives is quite active with Maybelle's House."

"Genevieve," I say. "I'm mostly helping with events at Mass General and the prison."

"Prison?" Margaret asks, surprised.

"Yes," I say, smiling. "I tutor inmates for their GED or college degrees."

"Wow, that's…very noble of you."

"Not noble, Margaret. I just believe in second chances. After all, I got one, right?"

She looks at me for a long moment, as if she can see underneath my skin, to all the moments and miracles and magic I've been clinging to since I was a little girl with a bald head and a devastating prognosis.

"I'm glad Theo has you, Sofia," she says it like she means it and the sentiment eases the remainder of my nerves over officially meeting her as Theo's girlfriend.

"I'm the lucky one. I'm glad to see you and Mr. Lawrence in Boston."

"Lance," she corrects.

"Lance," I repeat, picking up my coffee mug. "I made us dinner reservations. Do you like steak?"

"Please say Carters," Margaret leans forward.

I laugh. "Carters."

Margaret laughs with me.

I take a sip of my coffee, appreciating Margaret and our conversation more than she'll ever know. Don's mother didn't like me on sight and my high school boyfriend's mom worried that I'd get sick and die, constantly telling her son I wasn't a safe bet. But Margaret looks at me and sees me, not a woman from questionable stock or genes. Just a woman who cares for her son. The fact that that's enough for her makes me look forward to the tomorrows I usually block out.

Theo and Lance join us for a coffee, and we sit around the island, no frills, talking and laughing until it's time to freshen up for dinner. When Theo catches my eye, his dance, filled with happiness. I smile at him, reveling in this moment. The one where things click together.

I'm so excited for dinner with the Lawrence family, that I brush off Dad's text message, vowing to talk to him tomorrow instead.

DAD

Sofia, we need to talk. Please, call me when you have a chance.

CHAPTER 19
THEO

"You seem happy," Dad comments, holding out his hand.

I shake it, grinning. "I am."

We're in front of Carters Steakhouse, waiting for the valet to bring my SUV around. Dinner was better than I expected. While I'm used to my parents fawning over Heather and being completely engaged in my brother's relationship, I haven't brought a woman around in a long time. Not since Delphine. And even then, Mom and Dad never warmed up to her the way they naturally did with Sofia.

"Big game tomorrow night," Dad adds. "You ready?"

"Hope so. It feels like I've been waiting my whole career for this and now…" I trail off, my gaze snagging on Sofia as she and Mom make their way out of Carters. They stopped by the ladies' room on our way out and I can't tear my eyes away from the woman who makes me feel everything at once.

"It's nerve-wracking when it finally comes together, isn't it?" Dad asks.

"Too good to be true."

"Not when you've earned it, son."

"I've made a lot of mistakes," I remind him.

"We all have. Well, some more than others."

I crack a smile.

"But," he continues, "that's part of growing up."

"I guess."

Dad's hand finds my shoulder and rests there. He follows my line of vision. "Are we talking about hockey or Sofia?"

"Both." I shrug.

"You've been patient, Theo. Put in your time on the ice, with the team. You've worked hard to make amends for last season, and you earned this shot."

"Thanks, Dad."

"And with Sofia…"

I turn to look at him.

"Well, the way she looks at you matches the way you look at her, so I'd say, you guys deserve this moment. Enjoy it."

I tilt my head toward his in thanks. Sofia and Mom are only a few paces away when I remember I wanted to ask him about Ted Strauss. "Dad," I start but my words fall away when I catch Dad's expression. Something about it, or maybe something about the moment, stops me.

Sofia and Mom are laughing, their arms hooked together. Sofia looks so carefree. Mom looks younger, as if she hasn't enjoyed a conversation with another woman in years. Dad's expression is soft, the lines in his face smoothing out, as he stares at my mom like he still can't believe he married her.

For a minute, time stands still. I see Sofia and know that I'm falling in love with her. Because when I look at my parents, I can see our future so clearly. And I know that in thirty years' time, I'll be gazing at Sofia with the same admiration my dad has for Mom.

"Yeah, Theo?" Dad asks, his eyes still on Mom.

"It's nothing," I murmur, not wanting to ruin this moment. Somehow, I know that bringing up Sofia's father will change something. Will shatter this beautiful illusion of peace we've all wrapped ourselves in today.

"You sure?" Dad asks.

I nod, my smile widening as Sofia stops in front of me. "Positive." I lean down and kiss my girl's cheek.

"You better get home. Big day tomorrow," Mom reminds me, but she's looking at Sofia.

Sofia's expression softens and I realize Mom's referring to her hospital visit and not my game. The realization makes me happy; I like that Mom is concerned about Sofia. I like that Sofia trusted Mom enough to tell her about tomorrow.

"I'll drive you to your hotel," I offer.

Mom and Dad exchange another look.

"We're actually going to grab a glass of wine." Dad points to a small wine bar tucked away, almost hidden, beside Carters.

I groan and Sofia giggles.

"You sure?" This time, I ask Dad.

He chuckles. "Positive. You kids get home okay."

"Thank you for dinner, Lance and Margaret," Sofia says, kissing my parents goodbye.

"It was great getting to know you better," Dad tells Sofia.

Mom whispers something to Sofia that makes her smile widen.

"Good night, Mom." I kiss her cheek. "Dad." I shake his hand. "See you tomorrow."

"Sleep well, Theo," Mom murmurs.

Then she places her hand in Dad's and he leads her toward the wine bar they want to check out.

"Your parents are the best," Sofia says as my SUV arrives.

"They're pretty cool," I agree, tipping the valet and moving toward the driver's side.

When Sofia and I are buckled in, I pull out of the parking lot and point the SUV toward my condo. "Come home with me?" I plant my hand on Sofia's knee.

"I'd love to," she agrees. "Tomorrow's your big game."

"Tomorrow's your big test."

She wrinkles her nose. "Game day trumps doctor day."

I squeeze her knee and she squirms. "I can still come with you."

"No." She shakes her head. "You need to get in the right headspace for your season opener. And I need to do this on my own." She glances at me.

"Promise to call if you need me?" I ask, reluctant to let her spend the entire day at the hospital. Alone. But she even turned down Jesse's offer to sit with her.

"Promise." She grips my hand in hers and brings the back of my hand to her mouth, kissing it. "And I'll be at the game. Rocking your number."

"Hell yeah." I glance at her. "Thanks for making reservations, for wanting to spend time with my parents."

"Thanks for officially introducing me to them. They're really the loveliest couple I've ever met. Down-to-earth and just...sincere."

"Yeah, most people are surprised when they meet them. I think there's an expectation that they'll be haughty."

Sofia shrugs. "Your mom is very warm. Accepting. Is she like that with all your girlfriends?"

I chuckle, clenching her fingers before dropping her hand. "Is that your way of asking if I've had a lot of girls?"

Sofia's eyes twinkle and she shrugs. "Maybe."

"Well, I hate to sound lame but, I didn't. I mean, I didn't bring girls around. Just Delphine, who my parents weren't crazy about. And you, who they clearly adore."

"Why weren't they crazy about Delphine?" she asks, more curious than digging for information.

I sigh, chewing the corner of my mouth. "I think they could tell she was after more than just our relationship. From the get-go, they had a better read on her, on her motives, than I did. I've experienced it before, with friends or teammates, even teachers and coaches, but never with a girl I cared for. That's the only thing my parents don't tolerate."

"What?"

"Deception." I look at her, noting the severity of her expression. "They don't like being taken advantage of. Because chances are, if someone just asks for help, they're happy to do it."

Sofia nods. "It must be hard always feeling like people have a motive when they want to know you or spend time with you."

"Why do you think I went by Eddie for so long?"

"Yeah, I get it now."

"Good." I reach back over, linking our hands together. "Now that dinner is done…"

She bats her eyelashes at me. "Yes, Theodore. Take me home and have your way with me."

I laugh at her antics. But as her expression grows serious, my laughter falters. Anticipation floods through me and I can't wait to get her home. Underneath me. "I intend to, Sof."

When we arrive at my place, we hustle up to my condo. The door closes behind us and we stare at each other for a long moment. In her eyes, I read her desire, her longing, her yearning. And damn, I hope she sees the same need in mine. She toes off her heels as I pull my sweater over my head.

Sofia leaps into my arms and I catch her easily, walking us into my bedroom. Her lips fuse with mine before I clear the threshold and I stumble, pressing her up against the doorframe and holding her there.

I kiss her passionately, our tongues dueling together for a heady moment before she slows our kiss. More nips and licks, tastes that savor. Sofia's hands drop to my belt buckle as I drag my mouth down the column of her neck, pressing open-mouthed kisses to her shoulder. "Love you in this dress, baby. But let's lose it." I tug down the zipper until the dress is a pile at her feet.

She exhales shakily, her breasts pressing into my chest. The lace of her bra grazes my skin with each breath she takes. My hand skates up her bare leg, gripping the underside of her thigh as I grind into her, loving the way her eyes roll back in her head when she feels my hardness against her core.

"Bed?" I murmur.

"Now," she agrees.

I grin and pull her away from the wall. Instead, I lay her down in the center of my bed. I lose my pants and boxers. Sofia leans up on her elbows, rocking the shit out of the deep red bra and panties she's wearing. She watches me like I'm a piece of art, like she can't look away even though she can't fully figure me out.

"What is it?" I mutter, wanting to know all her thoughts.

The corners of her lips curve into a smile. "I know it's too soon but…I'm falling for you, Theo."

The words slam into me, bursting like water balloons, dousing me in a reality I was too scared to hope for. "Baby, I've already fallen." I tell her the truth. "You changed the game for me, Sofia."

Her eyes widen and the most beautiful smile crosses her face, lighting her up like a Christmas tree. "Come here." Her knees fall open, making room for me between her thighs.

I go willingly and settle between her legs. My fingers dust the tops of her shoulders, dragging down the straps of her bra. I kiss the tops of her breasts, her throat, jawline, and finally, her mouth. Her legs encircle my hips, her heels pressing into my back as she pulls me closer.

"Make me feel, Theo," she murmurs her regular command.

"Always, my baby." I dip my tongue into her mouth, and she sucks it before her eyes close, her mouth widens, and I kiss her with all the feelings swirling inside of me.

We come together fast and hard, reveling in each other's orgasms as we drift back to earth. But then I take her again, slow and languid. We trace each other's skin, memorize each other's bodies, and savor each other's kisses, falling more in love with every moment we spend together.

For the first time in my life, I feel fulfilled. Settled. Desperate to stay in a moment forever.

CHAPTER 20
SOFIA

The thundercloud rips open the following morning, pelting me with sheets of rain and gusts of wind.

Theo's already in the kitchen, blending up smoothies, when I pull myself from his bed.

"Sof, want a smoothie?" he calls out.

"Sure," I keep my voice even, flinching as the blender resumes its blending. The sound cuts through my anxiety as I make my way to the bathroom.

I use the toilet, my stomach twisting at the blood stain in my underwear. Something is fucking wrong; I know it.

I let out a shaky exhale and fold the underwear into a tiny square, stuffing it into my purse. Then, I take a hot shower, letting the steam fill the bathroom, dilute some of the worry now clogging the space.

I'm rinsing the conditioner from my hair when Theo appears on the other side of the glass.

"Hey." He grins his signature, sexy smirk. He shakes the glass filled with a purple smoothie, a straw bending over the top.

I force a smile. "You're spoiling me."

"How so?"

I turn off the shower and Theo holds out a towel.

"I know that has fro-yo in it," I joke as I step out of the shower. I wrap the towel around my frame, feeling the soft material against my skin with acute awareness. Suddenly, I feel hypersensitive. The steam is too thick, the bathroom light too harsh, the towel pressing into every nerve ending in my being. I cough to clear away the swell of emotion growing in my throat.

"Hey, hey, hey," Theo murmurs, placing the smoothie on the bathroom vanity. He wraps his arms around me, pulling me close. The wetness of my hair seeps through the cotton of his T-shirt, a growing stain I relate with all too well. "I know you're worried about today. Baby, everything is going to be fine. You got this, okay?"

I nod into his chest.

"Let me come with you, Sof." His voice cracks and I close my eyes, hating myself for hurting him. Knowing that the hurt is only going to get worse.

"I'll be fine." I sound strangled and Theo holds me closer. "I promise."

"Why won't you let me come?" he whispers.

I steady my breathing and pull back, hoping the redness in my face can be attributed to the steamy shower and not my emotional turmoil. "Tonight's your season opener."

"It doesn't matter."

"Of course, it does." I grip his wrist. "It matters, Theo. And I can't wait to cheer you on. Trust me, if you spend the day at the hospital, your energy stores will be so depleted, you won't have anything else to give for the game."

"You don't have to protect me; I want to be the one looking out for you."

I smile. "You are. Really. I just need...some peace of mind, okay?"

He nods slowly, his eyes steady on mine, but he doesn't look convinced.

"Can I have my smoothie now?"

"Yeah, Sof." He passes it to me. "Can I drive you?"

I glance at him over my shoulder as I lift the straw to my lips. The smoothie is cool and refreshing, centering. I know I need to give this incredible man something, so I nod. "Sure, Theo. That would be great."

He smiles and dips his chin before closing the bathroom door behind him.

I plop down on the toilet seat and close my eyes, trying to get my breathing under control. My head swims and my eyes burn. The condensation of the glass sweats against my palm.

I'll be fine. Everything will be okay. I got this.

But even as I repeat the words, I know they're a lie. Just like my thinking that this time would be any different.

My phone beeps and I swipe it off the vanity.

JESSE

I'll meet you at Mass Gen for breakfast. You can't say no. I'm bringing coffee.

I snort and release a shaky breath, clinging to wisps of humor with both hands.

SOFIA

I want a fancy one. From Starbucks.

My brother replies immediately.

JESSE

Too easy. Hey, Ted called but I missed it. He left a voicemail and wants you to call him back. I messaged him, let him know you're tied up at the hospital today. But you should reach out to him.

SOFIA

Yeah, thanks. I'll call him.

The ball in my throat grows at the mention of my dad. I know I need to call him. Last week, he was the one dodging calls, and this week, it's all me. But something keeps holding me back.

It's as if I know the moment I talk to Dad, the life I'm building will collapse. With today's long day of tests and appointments, I'm not in the right headspace to take on any more hopelessness.

A crash of thunder sounds in my mind and I close my eyes.

Then, I lie to myself.

I'll be fine. Everything will be okay. I got this.

I'M READING my third magazine when Dr. Jones pops his head into the waiting room.

"Sofia Carpenter." He smiles warmly, approaching me with an extended hand.

One of my nurses pointed him out earlier so I know the man with the friendly smile and greying hair is one of the leading oncologists in the Northeast.

"That's me." I shake his hand. "Good to meet you."

"Likewise. Why don't we head into my office and talk for a few?"

"Sure," I squeak out, my stomach twisted into the weaver's knots I associate with the antiseptic of hospitals and the cool blue paint color of the walls. A rush of longing for my mother floods through me and I clear my throat to hold my emotions in check.

Dr. Jones leads me to his office, and I slink through the door, holding my purse close against my stomach. I sink to one of the chairs across from his desk, my spine straight, my knees bouncing.

Dr. Jones settles behind his desk and places his fingertips together. He watches me over his steepled hands for a breath and the knots in my stomach become unbearably tight.

My eyes swing around his office, taking it all in. I note the golf memorabilia and photographs he has, several of him and a small girl, probably his daughter. I wet my lips and blurt out, "You like golf?"

Warmth seeps into his eyes as he nods, leaning back in his chair. "Yes. You play?"

"Not very well." I think back to the handful of rounds I played with Don in Maui. But that was from before. Before *this*. And still, only a few months ago. Time is strange like that, tricky and fickle. Unsuspecting and unassuming. Too many contradictions to process. I blow out a breath, my gaze catching on a suncatcher. I bet his daughter made that for him too. If I was his daughter, would he move mountains to save my life? Would he do the unthinkable?

Dr. Jones clears his throat and hunches forward again.

I don't meet his gaze. "How bad is it?"

"Is there someone we can call? A family member or a friend you'd like to be here?"

The back of my nose burns and a chill ripples down my spine. Mom and Mitch are on their cruise around the world; I think in Malta this week. Dad's in New Hampshire. Jesse and Theo will be heading to the arena soon, getting psyched up and ready for tonight's season opener.

"No," I say clearly, turning toward him. I clench the clasp of my purse. "It's okay, really. You can tell me. How bad is it?"

And then he says the words that once again change my life forever. They rock me to my core, alter the trajectory of everything I was planning for, and gut me from the inside out.

"Sofia, you have cancer."

The suncatcher sprays a prism of light over the floor of Dr. Jones's office and I latch onto it, unable to look away from the dancing colors and beams of light.

You have cancer.

I work another swallow, my throat suddenly parched. The ball of worry and nerves is gone, replaced instead by the quiet knowing that I was right. The thundercloud isn't a thundercloud anymore but a blizzard, pelting down hail and sleet.

"Sofia?" Dr. Jones's voice is gentle. Kind. "Is there someone we can call?"

His voice is too far away, as if I'm hearing it underwater. Under the blue-green sea in Maui, where a surfer once rode my heart all the way to the coastline.

The ringing of my phone startles us both. I stare down at my purse, still resting in my lap, my fingers tightly clutching the leather. I open it and pull out my phone, wincing as "Dad" flashes across the screen.

Dr. Jones clears this throat. "I'll give you a moment. Then, we can speak about your prognosis, treatment options, expectations."

"Sure," I murmur, knowing that everything we need to talk about is important. So unbelievably important, it's critical. But right now, I just want to hear my dad's voice. I want to sink into my mom's arms as she folds a thick wool-knitted blanket around my shoulders. I want my brother to tell me everything will be fine and Mitch to stand beside me, a quiet but constant pillar of strength. And I want Theo.

Theo. The game. Tonight.

My chest clenches painfully.

The ribbon of rainbow light dances and shifts as Dr. Jones slips from the room.

My phone rings again, another call from Dad.

This time, I press accept and raise the phone to my ear. "Daddy," my voice breaks.

"Sofia, I'm in the lobby," Dad says. Tears stream down my cheeks because he knew. He knew I'd need him and he's here for me, ready to make another sacrifice if it will keep me healthy.

If it will buy me another second chance.

CHAPTER 21
THEO

I can taste the energy of the crowd, a shot of pure adrenaline that races through my veins, giving me the same type of high I feel when I'm with Sofia.

Invincible. Undefeatable. Worthy.

It's the third period and the Hawks are down by one goal, but I know that's about to change. I know it as surely as I knew Sofia would change my life. There's a certainty riding in my abdomen, a sureness in the glide of my skates, a confidence in the way I handle the stick.

The referee drops the puck and Austin gains control, maneuvering around Atlanta's center as I skate toward the net. From the corner of my eye, I clock Cap's posture. It's as if I can decipher the thoughts in his head, anticipate the way he's going to play this out. Sure enough, he passes me the puck and I'm off, keeping it controlled as I gain on the net. I outmaneuver Atlanta's defenseman like it's something I do every day, with an ease I never possessed until this moment.

Is it because of Sofia? Her belief in me and my ability to be the teammate, the player, I've always thought I'd grow into? Is it because I've finally come clean with the team about my name and my family? Or maybe because Mom and Dad are cheering in the stands and for the first time, I'm not trying to conceal that fact?

Whatever the reason, I know the second I snap my wrist and my stick connects with the puck, driving it straight toward the net, that I'm going to score. A moment later the goal horn blares and a cheer rings out, deafening in its volume, fulfilling in its intensity.

I pick my parents out in the stands and grin, loving how hard Dad claps and how Mom hops up and down, her hands dancing with the beat of the crowd. I frown when I don't see Sofia and for a second, a blaze of panic rushes through me.

But then Easton is smacking my back and Cap is hollering in my ear. I clear my head and focus back on the game, my team, winning. After eight minutes of hard play, I score again, putting the Hawks in the lead. We win three minutes later, and the crowd is raucous. Team morale is at an all-time high. I finally feel like I've redeemed myself with the men I admire most.

"That was some hell of a backhand," East says, complimenting my last shot on goal.

"Thanks, man," I toss back.

"Good game, Lawrence." Austin smacks my back.

"Hell yeah, dude!" Panda tosses an arm around my shoulder. "A game like this calls for—"

"Don't say shots," James Ryan laughs.

"Definitely shots," Panda concludes.

I snicker, moving along with the team toward the locker room. The bustle is tremendous, reporters, players, staff all milling about with huge smiles on their faces. I've been on the other end of this type of scene for years, but being at the center of it, being in the midst of it all, is a feeling I'll never forget.

Dad says I've earned this. But the truth is, I've been hungry for it for so long, I'm more relieved than anything that it's finally happening. I can't wait to tell Sofia, to see her face, to kiss her hard.

"Nice job out there." Yaeger grins.

"You too, man."

"Feels good, doesn't it?" he asks, understanding perfectly all the feelings coursing through me.

"The fucking best," I agree.

Yaeger laughs and slaps my shoulder. "We're heading to Taps. Tell your parents, grab your girl, it's time for—"

"SHOTS!" Panda hollers.

"Shots," Yaeger and I agree.

"YOU WERE PHENOMENAL!" Mom greets me with a beaming smile.

"I can't believe we haven't met your parents until now," Yaeger mutters. But then he turns his charming Southern drawl on Mom, and she practically melts into him and Vivi and their happy baby news.

"Good game, son." Dad holds out a hand, slapping me on the back. He leans closer, dropping his voice. "You've been letting me win at tennis all these years, haven't you? Because your speed on the ice…"

I chuckle, shrugging. "We'd be unstoppable as a double," I remind him.

He laughs. "True. We'll stick Preston with Harry next time."

I glance around for Sofia but don't see her in the hallway overflowing with family and friends. Some people are already moving toward the arena's exits. Where is she?

I find Jesse milling about, his phone glued to his ear, his

hand pressed over his other ear. He shuffles toward a corridor, probably searching for quiet.

"Dad, give me a second?"

"Sure," Dad says, pulled into the conversation Mom is having with Vivi. But he shoots me a glance and I see the concern in his eyes, the worry that something is amiss.

My natural high over winning the game dissipates as I follow Jesse. By the time I catch up with him, sitting on a bench, his posture defeated, his head hanging low, I feel nauseous.

"What's going on, man?" I ask.

He looks up, his eyes rimmed in red.

Fuck. I sink down next to him on the bench.

Jesse swears and shakes his head.

"Was that Sofia?" I ask, pointing to his phone. I know it's fucking awful, but I suddenly hope he got bad news about someone else, anyone else. Just not Sofia.

"Her mom," he mutters. "She and my dad are on their way back from Malta." He releases a shaky exhale and looks at me, his expression stricken. "Sofia's test results weren't what we hoped. She has cervical cancer."

"Wh-what?" I stutter. "No, that doesn't make any sense. She's healthy, fine, she's—"

"Sick," Jesse cuts in. "I know it's hard to process. I know it doesn't seem that way when she's so vibrant, outgoing. But Sofia is sick," he repeats, as if saying the words will somehow convince us both that they're true.

"Where is she?" I jump up, my fingers already closing around the car keys in my jacket pocket.

"She's with her dad."

"Her dad?" I repeat. "But doesn't he live in New Hampshire?"

"Yeah." Jesse stands next to me. "Listen, I don't know all the details. But right now, you should probably wait for Sofia to reach out to you."

"Fuck that." I glare at him, pissed that he would even suggest something so stupid. Like I won't be there for my girl. Like I won't do every goddamn thing in my power to make sure she feels safe, protected, loved.

"I'm not saying it to be a dick," Jesse replies. He looks too tired to battle with me right now, and at his expression, some of the fight building in my body releases. "I'm saying she's going to need you. A lot. But she's probably spinning right now, her mind going in a million different directions. Just, give her a few hours. Let her have this time with her dad. She'll hit you up and if not, I will."

I don't like it. In fact, I fucking hate it. But as I stare at a devastated Jesse, I realize he just wants what's best for his sister. He's not clamoring to her bedside even though I know he's desperate to be with her. He's putting her best interests first which unfortunately, don't coincide with his. Or mine.

"All right," I agree, my tone cracking.

Jesse holds out a hand, but I pull him in for a hug, smacking him hard on the back. "You'll let me know if anything—"

"I'll call you," he promises, releasing me.

I watch him walk away, a sense of foreboding, of helplessness, of goddamn agony burning through me. When the corridor door closes behind Jesse, the anger I kept at bay resumes, flaring into an inferno.

How the hell could my girl be sick? How didn't I see it? Know it?

It's illogical and yet, a part of me feels like I've failed her. I should have known something was…up. I think back over the past few weeks. She's been exhausted but I attributed that to her establishing a new life in Boston. She's complained of back pain but that could be from working out and taking pole-dancing classes.

The blood, the spotting, after sex blares in my mind.

Cervical fucking cancer. But it was just that first time and Sofia didn't seem concerned about it so I just…let it go.

I let it go and now my girl is laid up in a hospital with cervical fucking cancer.

The hospital! If anyone has connections with hospitals, it's my parents. Right now, I'm prepared to use every single one of them to make sure Sofia gets the best care, sees the best doctors, has the best odds and options at her fingertips.

With renewed purpose, I stride back toward my parents.

The moment Mom sees my face, she knows something is wrong. She politely extricates herself from the conversation and within moments, Mom, Dad, and I are in the parking lot of The Meadows, standing beside my SUV.

"What's going on?" Dad asks.

I shake my head. "Not here."

Dad holds out his hand and I drop my keys into his palm. My head is all over the place; I am the last person who should be behind a wheel. But how did Jesse get home? Or did he go straight to the hospital? I pull out my phone, frustrated he hasn't called or messaged yet.

"Theodore," Mom's voice is gentle. She guides me toward the passenger seat and pushes me into the SUV.

"Where to?" Dad asks once Mom is sitting behind me.

"I don't know," I admit.

"What happened?" Mom asks.

I turn to look at her, noting the worry in her expression.

"It's Sofia," I manage to say, my voice breaking. "She's sick."

CHAPTER 22
SOFIA

"She should get a hysterectomy," Dad whispers to Mom, who is keeping her composure quite well for someone who just traveled for fifteen hours straight.

"A hysterectomy? What if she wants to bear children?" Mom replies.

"Children? She may never get the chance to be a mother at all if she doesn't go through with this surgery. She needs to take a radical approach." Dad's voice shakes, partly with emotion and partly with conviction.

"What does Dr. Jones think?" Mitch cuts in.

I almost smile. Thank God for Mitch, always keeping the peace, always on my side.

"Don't you think we should get a second opinion?" Jesse this time. Of course my brother is here instead of sleeping off a hangover after a night celebrating the Hawks win. His first win as an NHL player. A win firmly secured by Theo's incredible play last night.

I pick up my phone, a knot in my throat as I scroll through the missed calls and unanswered messages from Theo. We need to talk; I know we do. But after yesterday's news and talking to my dad, I don't know what the hell to say.

If I didn't think I could forgive him after he flipped me a different name and career in Maui, there's no chance in hell he can forgive me now. If I felt deceived, he'll feel pure betrayal.

I close my eyes, recalling my conversation with Dad.

He entered Dr. Jones's office, his eyes wide with worry, his hair unkempt from dragging his fingers through it.

I stand, rushing him and throwing my arms around his waist.

"What is it?" he murmurs, knowing immediately that it's more than my annual tests. It's the unspeakable thing we try not to think about, but it hovers as a shadow in our minds all the time anyway.

"Cervical cancer," I murmur.

Dad swears and I feel the strength of his body physically leave as he sags forward, my words delivering a knockout blow. We sit in the chairs in front of Dr. Jones's desk, our hands linked, our eyes both devoid of and bleeding with emotion.

"What are you doing here? You hate the city," I remind him.

"I have to tell you something," Dad murmurs.

"And it couldn't wait," I snort, my gaze darting around the office.

I feel strangely shell-shocked, as if I'm watching myself and Dad have this conversation from outside of my body. From the periphery.

"Theo Lawrence," Dad says gravely.

I swing my eyes to his. "What about him?"

"Are his parents Lance and Margaret Lawrence?"

I nod. "They're lovely people."

Dad scoffs and dips his head. "They own the hospital that did the clinical trial for your leukemia."

A chill rushes through me as his words take root in my stomach, branch out into a tree of disbelief. "What?"

"They own the hospital that—"

"I heard you," I snap, dropping his hand to clutch the armrest. "Are you saying that Theo's parents own the hospital that wouldn't accept me into their clinical trial?"

"Yes. Because you didn't meet the requirements," Dad says carefully.

"What are you talking about? You said the trial was full." I gape at him.

"I lied," Dad winces, pain in his voice.

"I thought there was a last-minute cancellation," I blabber on.

"Sofia, do you think I would have gone to jail for insurance fraud for trying to get you into someone else's place after a last-minute cancellation?"

"You went to jail for trying to move me up the list," I state, but my voice wavers. Suddenly, I'm not so sure. How the hell don't I know the specifics about my dad's jail time? The logistics behind his sacrifice.

"I went to jail for fudging your test results."

"What?" I gasp.

Dad shakes his head. "Sofia, you are my blood. My life. I'd do anything to keep you safe. To keep you alive. But I committed health insurance fraud. I'd do the same damn thing all over again if it gave you a shot. But the people I lied to, the hospital I caused all that negative press for, it was Theo's family's."

Shock. Confusion. Hurt. It all blazes through me, an inferno of doubt.

A rap on the door sounds, followed by Dr. Jones's voice. "Are we ready to talk treatment options?"

Dad and I sit in silence until I finally nod.

Dr. Jones settles back behind his desk and begins to rattle off statistics, medications, fertility options. But I don't hear a word he says.

I don't hear anything at all.

And because of that, Mom, Dad, Mitch, and Jesse are currently standing in the hallway discussing my future, my treatment, like it's their decision to make.

What everyone conveniently forgot is I'm not eight years old this time. I'm twenty-four, a woman. One who believe in miracles and magic.

And feeling alive.

"HEY." Jesse pops his head into my room.

I'm already settled into the hospital, here for the next few days while tests are conducted, and results are analyzed. Then, the treatment will begin.

Mom and Mitch want to take me back to Michigan. Dad wants concrete answers to every question he has. Jesse wants to know what I want.

And Theo…Theo just wants me to call him back.

But I can't. What will I say to him? What if he hates me now?

He told me the one thing his parents won't accept is deception…and my family sure as hell did that.

"How are you holding up?" Jesse sits in the chair beside my bed, kicking his feet up on the bed frame.

"Oh, you know. Reading some literature," I joke, fanning myself with pamphlets that outline different treatment options. Chemotherapy, radiation, cone biopsy, radical trachelectomy, and the list goes on.

Jesse pins his lips together, nodding along. But I know this is hard for him. Seeing me this way guts him and I hate that he's hurting. "You talk to Theo?"

"Nope."

"Why not? If he's blowing up your phone half as much as he's blowing up mine, then it's a lot. It's not him holding back, it's you. What gives?"

"You hear about my dad?"

"That he wants you to get a hysterectomy?" Jesse asks.

I roll my eyes. "You know I could hear everything you all said in the hallway."

"I know. I also know you're going to do whatever you want too."

"Exactly."

"So I want to know where your head's at. Why won't you give Theo the time of day?" Jesse crosses his arms over his chest, waiting.

"All these years, I thought my dad went to jail for trying to pull strings, get me up a list faster into an empty spot in the clinical trial."

"Yeah," Jesse agrees, frowning. Well, that's a relief. For as much as I was kept in the dark, so was he. I don't know how many more betrayals I can handle and one from Jesse would devastate me.

"Apparently, that's not the case."

"What happened?" Jesse leans forward, his elbows dropping to his knees.

I take a deep breath and fill him in on the details. When I'm done, his eyes are blown, his mouth hanging open.

"You're shitting me."

"I wish."

"The hospital your dad almost brought down, with all that talk of shady dealings and fraud, belongs to Theo's parents?"

"That about sums it up," I say, keeping my voice light when my body feels like lead. My dad deceived Theo's parents. Not only his parents, but the doctors and scientists running the trial. Not only them but me.

He did all of that to save my life and for that…I can't even be mad. Because if I didn't get into that clinical trail, I'm ninety-nine percent certain I'd be dead. That trial, the combination of medication introduced, is when I started to turn a corner. It's the thing that pushed me onto a path of healing, toward remission.

And now I'm back in the hospital, this time with a different diagnosis, and a very different worldview.

Still, I'm not mad. More hurt than anything. Maybe a little bit distraught since it's time to face facts.

I've got a long road ahead of me, recovery wise. I may lose my ability to bear children. And I've got zero chance of making this work with Theo. Not when my family hurt his. Not when my future is so uncertain. Not when the thought of his disappointment slices me up inside.

"You should call him," Jesse says, accurately reading my mind.

"I don't know what to say."

"How about the truth?"

I scoff. "I'm sure he's already figured it out."

"Is that why you're avoiding his calls?"

I narrow my eyes at Jesse.

He glares right back at me. "Never took you to be fearful."

"Yeah well, you've never sat in this bed before," I spit back, immediately regretting the words. Because they're unfair and driven by frustration and fear more than truth. "I'm sorry."

"Don't be." Jesse shakes his head. "I'm not offended. Because you're right. I've never been where you are, and if I could, I'd switch places with you in a heartbeat."

"That's not what I meant," I backpedal, trying to clarify.

"I know; it's what I meant. But even though I've never been where you are, I've been by your side as you've tried to come to terms with your illness, your childhood, your dad, all of it. And I know you live in moments; you find yourself in the space between heartbeats and the seconds of silence the rest of us take for granted. You don't back down from experiences when you could feel them all instead. You're no regrets, no bullshit. Don't lose that now, Sofia. Cause that's something you will regret."

His words take my breath away, making it hard to form thoughts.

"I'm going to grab a water. You want anything?" He stands and I shake my head.

When Jesse's gone, I replay his words over and over in my mind.

You live in moments.

You find yourself in the space between heartbeats.

Don't back down from experiences.

No regrets. No bullshit.

No bullshit. Isn't that what I asked of Theo?

I squeeze my eyes shut tight.

Sometimes I hate when I'm right, if only because it means I have to take my own advice.

CHAPTER 23
THEO

"Ted Strauss's daughter," Mom repeats, flabbergasted.

Dad nods, pouring Mom another cup of tea.

"She didn't know," Mom decides, her voice firm.

Dad and I both stare at her, wondering if she means the words or is just trying to convince herself.

In the past, Mom has always proved a wonderful judge of character. She was the first person who pegged Delphine for who she really was. And while I don't want to believe that Sofia knew of her father's connection to my parents, I can't dismiss it until she speaks to me. Why won't she call me back? Or answer my messages? Why won't she tell me how she's doing? Or what she needs from me?

I lace my fingers behind my head and pace next to the kitchen island, the questions with no answers on a loop in my mind.

"She didn't know," Mom repeats, waiting for confirmation from Dad and me.

"No, I don't think she knew who I—" I start but then stop. Didn't she know my true identity from the beginning, right from that first night in Maui? Theo Lawrence. I never hid my real name from her, just my hockey persona. "Maybe she didn't know the full story behind her dad."

Dad gives me a skeptical look. "Sofia didn't know her dad went to jail for insurance fraud?"

"She did. But she told me he went to jail for the right reason," I offer up.

"Well, saving her life is the right reason," Mom cuts in. "We would have done the same thing for you or Preston if we believed it was our only option."

Dad closes his eyes and sighs.

"We would have," Mom repeats, more forcefully this time.

Dad nods.

"It doesn't add up," Dad offers. "When she met us, she was sincere."

"Her stepfather, Mitch Carpenter, adopted her. She took his last name. I thought that was weird, and when I asked her about it, she shrugged it off. Said it was her father's idea, that he wanted her to have a fresh start."

"Could be," Dad says after a long moment. "No man wants their kid to have a different man's name if it's not for the kid's benefit."

"Have you heard from her?" Mom asks quietly.

I shake my head. "That's the thing that bothers me. If there's nothing to hide, then why is she avoiding me?"

"She could just be processing. A cancer diagnosis is a lot to swallow," Mom murmurs.

"I know." I close my eyes. What's wrong with me, making this about me, or Sofia and me, when it needs to be about her. Her options and resources and future. "What can we do?"

Dad shakes his head. "Nothing, until she agrees. We can't just arrange for doctors to meet her if she's not willing to meet with them."

"But it's for her own good," I argue.

"I know," Dad agrees.

Mom smiles gently. "Now you can understand why Ted

went to the lengths he did. When you love someone, you'll do anything to keep them safe."

Her words slam into me like a truth bomb. She's right. For years, I couldn't stand all the people who tried to take advantage of me or my family because of our last name. I blamed the negative press surrounding the hospital and the clinical trial for my parents' step back from public life. For my need to go by Eddie Sims in the hockey world.

But the truth is, Mom and Dad are no different than Ted Strauss. They're all parents, who will do whatever needs to be done to keep their kids safe. And Mom and Dad have been a lot happier since keeping a quieter lifestyle. I've certainly enjoyed being Eddie, of knowing that my hockey career was built by my hard work and performance instead of the legacy of being a Lawrence.

"I know what Ted Strauss did was wrong," I say quietly. "I know it compromised the reputation of the hospital. I know it cost a lot of money. I know it nearly upended the clinical trial. I know all that and yet…"

"You can't help but understand why he made the decision he did?" Dad asks.

I nod.

"I know," Dad says quietly, picking up a mug and taking a sip of his coffee. "Trust me, I stayed awake a lot of nights during that time. It was awful, having to take legal action against a man whose decisions you could understand. Hell, I'd make the same ones if I was in his place. Desperate to save my kid, wanting to give them every option. But we couldn't let it go, Theo." Dad stares right at me. "You know that, right? We couldn't just pretend that health insurance fraud didn't take place even though we wished we could have."

"I know," I murmur. Of course my parents couldn't discredit the entire hospital for one case. How many other patients would have lost care? How many doctors and nurses and hospital staff would have lost jobs if the hospital shut down?

No, they did what they had to do. Ted Strauss did what he had to do.

And now, I need to do what I need to do.

I pick up my jacket off the back of a barstool and tug it on. "I need to see her."

Mom and Dad nod, unsurprised.

"I'll call you," I offer.

Mom hugs me tight. "We've extended our stay, so we'll be at the hotel. Let us know however we can help."

"I will." I kiss her goodbye. Glancing at my parents, I say, "Thank you."

Dad nods and walks me to the door. Then, I head to my SUV and point it in the direction of the hospital. It's time Sofia and I talked. No bullshit.

SEEING my girl in a hospital bed, her dark hair piled on top of her head, her face pale is like being kicked in the nuts. It's fucking brutal, painful on a level I can't describe unless someone else has had a similar experience.

Yaeger comes to mind and a surge of guilt for what I caused him and Vivi to experience last season rushes through me.

"Hey, baby." I rap my knuckles against her open hospital room door.

She glances up and the moment her eyes lock on mine, emotions blaze through them. As I cross the threshold, it bleeds out, replaced with a wariness that lands like a second kick to the nuts.

"You lose my number?" I say it as a joke but the hurt in

my tone is too obvious to play off as anything but a real question. *Why have you been avoiding me? Why are you icing me out?*

Instead of grinning, Sofia's eyes fill with tears, and I drop into the chair beside her bed, feeling awful. "I was joking," I backtrack.

"No, you weren't." She tries for a smile.

"I want to talk."

"I know."

"How are you? What's your prognosis? I only know what Jesse tells me and I assure you, it's not the whole story. Please, Sof, let me in. Tell me what's up," I plead, wishing I could lay down beside her and wrap her in my arms. Her body, always so in sync with mine, is stiff. Unyielding.

She rolls her lips together, turning toward me. Sofia releases a long exhale. "Here's what I know," she begins. Then, she tells me all about her diagnosis and the symptoms she was experiencing.

"Bleeding after sex?" I cut in.

She nods. "That's the main one that should have clued me in."

"But it was only one time. The first time," I remind her. She averts her gaze and my stomach sinks. "Why didn't you tell me?"

"I don't know," she murmurs. "Maybe because I knew, deep down, that it was something. Or maybe because I didn't want to ruin us when it was so, so good."

"It's still good, baby," I say, a new fear anchoring in my chest. Why the hell is she speaking in the past tense? Does she think we can't get back what we had? Does she think we're over?

"I'm going for a surgery."

"What kind of surgery? When?" Suddenly, it feels like too much. Too real. Choices have been made, decisions finalized. I'm not saying I should have been included in them but...

didn't Sofia want to talk it out with me? Sort out her thoughts by confiding in me? "Sofia."

"A radical vaginal trachelectomy," she says easily. "It's where they'll go in and remove my cervix, nearby tissue, and dissect the lymph nodes as well to make sure the cancer hasn't spread."

I manage to swallow against the boulder crawling up my throat, constricting my ability to breathe. "What about radiation? Chemo?"

"We're holding off on it for now. If it's necessary afterwards, well, I'll make a decision then."

"Okay," I say slowly, at a loss of what to ask. What do I say? How can I best support Sofia?

"I picked this option because I want to preserve fertility," she admits, her eyes holding mine. They're searching and that scares the shit out of me. Does she find what she needs in my eyes? Or is my bewilderment pushing her further away?

"That's good then, right? That you have options that allow you to do that?" I sputter, so fucking far out of my comfort zone.

"It is," she agrees.

I nod, wracking my brain for what to say next. When I got in the car to drive over here, I thought we'd pick up where we left off. Sure, there would be things to discuss. Of course, it would be hard and painful. But not like this.

Not the awkward tension, this strange dance of not knowing how to be around each other when everything between Sofia and me was always so natural. Effortless.

"Are you going to address the elephant in the room?" she whispers, as if reading my mind. That gives me a sliver of comfort because maybe we still got this, maybe we can navigate our way forward. Forward and together.

"I don't care about anything except you," I say truthfully. Suddenly, all this shit from the past, her dad, the clinical trial, my parents, none of it matters. "As soon as I walked in this room and saw you, I realized just how much nothing matters but you. Me and you."

Sadness sweeps her expression. She tries to smile but it falls, and tears fill her eyes. "My dad committed fraud."

"I don't care."

"I didn't know."

"It doesn't matter," I reiterate. Even if she had known, it wouldn't change how I feel about her. "People do things sometimes to survive. Because they don't see another way. Not everything is black and white, Sof."

"Cancer is. You either have it or you don't. I have it, Theo. It's not going anywhere. The thundercloud will always hover over my head."

"Then I'll stand under it with you."

She shakes her head. "That's not the life you want. Trust me, it's not the life anyone wants. We're not married, we don't have children. You don't need to make that kind of sacrifice. No one else should have to sacrifice their life, their freedom, for me. My dad already did that and I gotta tell you, the guilt is hard to handle. I don't want to shoulder anyone else's burden."

"It's my choice," I remind her. My chest twists, knowing she's taking that away from me, if only to safeguard herself. And how the hell can I be angry with her about that? When she has so much on her plate? When she's handling all of this —every damn thing—with so much maturity. Rationality. Even grace.

"I know," she admits softly, looking down. When she glances back up, her eyes are blown with emotions, all swimming in chocolate depths. "I swear to you, I didn't know who your parents were. I didn't know the full story of my dad and the clinical trial. I didn't know who you really were in relation to my family and my past."

"I believe you," I rush out, wondering if this is the issue she's hung up on. Haven't I already made it clear that it doesn't matter? "Nothing can change the way I feel about you."

A tear tips over, slips silently down her cheek. "I love you for that, Theo. I love everything about you."

"I love you too, Sof. More than you even comprehend."

"But I can't do this with you anymore," her voice breaks, cracking my chest in the process.

"What are you talking about? Baby, I'm not going anywhere."

"I'm asking you to. I know the truth now, Theo. I know how hard it was for you to feel like people were taking advantage of you. It affected you so deeply that you pretty much changed your name, your identity."

"What happened with Delphine—"

"It wasn't Delphine, Theo," Sofia interrupts, shaking her head. "It was my dad. What my dad did changed the trajectory of your life, of your parents' work."

"He did it to save your life!" I blurt out.

"It doesn't make it right," she says quietly, staring at her hands.

What the hell is happening right now? Sofia isn't making any sense. "Sofia—"

"I can't do this with you anymore. Not knowing what I know. Not when I have to focus on getting better, on trying to beat this. I look at you and feel guilty. Feel…icky. That my family deceived yours."

"Sofia," my tone is desperate, pleading. I need her to understand that nothing matters except her. Why doesn't she get that?

"Please, Theo." She closes her eyes, pained and exhausted. "I don't want to argue with you. I just want to get through this surgery."

"When is it?" I ask.

"Four days."

"I'll be here," I promise.

She shakes her head and opens are eyes. "We haven't been together that long. Our pasts, the intersection of our pasts, is too complicated. What we had was the most beautiful thing in my life but what's coming next will destroy everything beautiful. So please, let me go. Focus on hockey, be with your family, and keep growing into the Theo I fell in love with. And let me beat this."

My cheeks are wet, and it takes me a second to realize I'm crying. When was the last time I cried? "You're breaking my heart, Sof." I tell her the truth, the physical ache rivaling the mental anguish.

"It will heal stronger," she assures me, smiling through her own tears. "Thank you for a beautiful dream, Theo."

"I'm still not going anywhere." I don't give a shit what she wants; I'll be in that waiting room in four days. I'll hound her brother for updates; I won't walk away from her. Or give up on us.

"But I am," she murmurs.

I frown, not understanding the intent behind her words.

"Oh good, you're awake." A nurse interrupts waltzing into the room, oblivious that my entire world just shifted. Broke. "We're going to run some tests now." She starts fiddling with Sofia's IVs.

"Okay," Sofia says, shooting me a soft smile. "Take care of yourself." She says it like she's finishing up lunch with an acquaintance. Like she didn't just rip my heart from my chest. Like the past few weeks of us practically living together haven't meant anything at all.

I nod and watch as the nurse helps her into a wheelchair and takes her down the hallway.

Hurt burns me from the inside out but I'm still not going anywhere. Sofia can be scared and hurt and confused.

But for the first time in my life, I'm going to be strong enough for the both of us.

CHAPTER 24
SOFIA

Being in the hospital brings flashbacks from my childhood. Mom's swollen eyes and her knitting. Dad's appearing as a ghost of himself, introverted and lost to his own thoughts.

But it's different this time. Because Mitch and Jesse are part of my family now too. Plus, I'm older, able to understand my options, able to advocate for myself. Mom's knitting needles have reappeared, and Dad is definitely speaking less, but they're also handling my prognosis calmer than when I was a child.

Every day, Dad hangs out, bringing crossword puzzles and fresh coffee. Mom's made me a new scarf and loaded up my bedside table with romance novels. The feel good, happy kind. Mitch likes to swing by in the afternoon, when he knows I need an energy pick-me-up. And Jesse, well, he's in and out as his hockey schedule allows.

The morning after my visit from Theo, I'm still in low spirits, wallowing in self-pity.

"I know you're devastated that I'm heading out of town, but you don't have to cry about it," my brother says, entering my hospital room with a green tea for me.

I snort, rolling my eyes. I've been pricked and prodded, whisked to tests and am on several IV drips. In one week, my life flipped upside down and I'm still processing the fallout.

"What's going on?" Jesse asks casually but I hear the undercurrent of concern in his tone.

"I tried to break up with Theo."

"Tried to?" He leans forward.

"He says he's not going anywhere."

"He's a smart guy." Jesse shrugs, leaning back in his chair, satisfied with this response.

"Are you not listening? You're supposed to be on my side," I remind him.

"Not when you're self-sabotaging your own happiness," my brother remarks, logical. And annoying.

"I'm not self—"

"Yes, you are. You feel guilty because of your dad's connection to the Lawrences. You think that that experience changed things for Theo, how he chose to live his life, yada, yada."

"It's not yada, yada. He changed his name."

This time my brother rolls his eyes. "Cut the shit, Sofia. You're scared."

"Damn right I'm scared," I hiss at Jesse. "I'm getting my cervix removed in three fucking days."

My brother's expression sobers, and he shifts in his chair, not uncomfortable, more…convinced. He lifts his eyebrows. I narrow my gaze back.

"What?" I say after a moment. "You're annoying me."

He cracks a grin. "I always annoy you. And I get why you're scared. That's a normal reaction. Hell, even pushing Theo away is a normal reaction since I have no clue how the hell you're feeling or processing or how you should react. But Sofia, Theo's all fucking in with you. He has been from the jump. You really think he gives a shit about the past? About his parents and your dad and whatever happened a decade ago? He cares about you!"

I shake my head. "I can't do that to him again."

"Do what?"

"Deceive him."

"You're not. That ship has sailed, Sofia. It's done and in the past. This is now, this is new."

I close my eyes. "What if I don't make it? What if I make it and can't have kids? What if I make it and in three years, it comes back?"

"What if, Sofia? What if Theo busts his knee and is out for the season? What if he gets a concussion and can't play hockey? What if he can't have kids? Would that make you want to be with him any less?"

"It's not the same thing!" I lose my patience and lash out at Jesse.

I can tell from his expression that he's not enjoying this but he's also not backing down. Jesse is the only person in my family who gives me tough love and even though I know that's what he's doing, his timing is all wrong.

"I know," he admits quietly. "I know it's not the same. I'm not trying to reduce your cancer to hockey or anything trivial. I'm trying to point out, to make you see, that life is all what-ifs. You're making the past part of the present, letting it dictate your future. And that's not you, Sofia. You're all about the moment, remember? The now. There isn't space in the now for what if. When did you forget that?"

Tears well in my eyes as my feelings for Theo mix with my frustration over the situation I'm in with Theo. "I understand what you're saying, Jes. But right now, it's too much. Right now, I need to focus on this week. The surgery."

"Okay," Jesse agrees, his tone softer. He pulls back on his tough love and gives me his hand, effortlessly switching into compassionate brother mode. "Just don't give up on yourself, Sofia."

"I'm not."

"What do you need right now?"

I give him a pathetic smile and glance at the green tea he brought me. "Coffee would be a good start."

Jesse tosses back his head and laughs before getting to his feet. "You got it."

When he exits the room, my ability to remain calm and somewhat unaffected goes with him. The tears come, first in streams and then in waves. I can't drag Theo through this when I'm still trying to process it all. I can't shackle him to a life of uncertainty, of most likely needing to lean into the benefits his last name provides, when he swore he never wanted that. I just need to get through this surgery. As guilt-free as possible.

"WE COME BEARING GIFTS," Vivi announces, entering my hospital room with a tray filled with sweet treats. Cupcakes, cookies, chocolate-dipped Oreos.

"It's like the last supper," I joke.

Claire laughs but Vivi, Chloe, and Abbi look unsure of how to react.

"I kid." I grin. "Okay, too soon."

"Way too soon," Chloe agrees, sitting down beside me. She places a coffee on my bedside table. "Jesse told us tea is out and coffee is in."

I laugh, recalling our conversation from yesterday.

"This is a much better way to watch hockey," Abbi agrees, taking a gulp of her Starbucks beverage and dragging a chair closer to my bedside.

Claire swipes my rolling tray table to set up a large laptop screen and pull up the hockey game. "Indy sends her love.

She wanted to come hang tonight, but Emmaline isn't feeling great."

"It's no worries. This is pretty cool, guys," I admit, appreciating how much effort they went through to hang out with me and not have it be awkward. Clearly, watching Boston play against Edmonton in an away game is something that would gather this little group together. Right now, I appreciate their willingness to watch the game from the discomfort of my hospital room more than they'll ever know.

"Right?" Vivi agrees, biting into a chocolate-covered Oreo. "Oh my God, this is so good. Y'all, I can't stop eating sweets."

"That means you're having a girl." Chloe points at her.

"Better hope you don't end up with gestational diabetes," Abbi comments.

We all look at her but Claire and Vivi laugh.

"What?" Abbi asks. "One of Luca's sisters had it with her last pregnancy and she said it sucked."

Vivi reaches for another cookie. "Better enjoy this while I still can," she quips.

I smile and rest back against my pillows.

"Your surgery is in two days?" Chloe asks.

"Yep," I respond. "They really moved things around to accommodate me given my previous history."

"You don't know, do you?" Claire looks at me thoughtfully.

"Know what?" I ask, a drip of concern dropping into my stomach.

"Claire," Abbi warns.

"Eddie's, I mean Theo's—the whole name thing is still tripping me up. Anyway, his parents are well connected with this hospital. Theo demanded that you have the best team on whatever time schedule was in your best interest," she explains.

"No way," I refute it immediately, shaking my head. "Theo doesn't know my case, my past. He—"

"He wasn't privy to any specifics. Just that you get what you need, what you want, and when you want it. That your doctors speak to you directly and understand your concerns and needs. He wants you to have the best resources at your disposal," she adds.

"But…how do you know that?" I ask, confused.

Claire blushes.

Abbi scoffs, "Claire's eavesdropping skills are—"

"Unparalleled," Claire cuts her off. "I overheard Theo talking to Easton and Austin the other day. They were at the house, watching game tape, and I was…you know."

"Eavesdropping?" Vivi grins. "I love it." She turns toward me. "What's the deal with y'all anyway?"

"Me and Theo?" I ask, stalling.

Vivi arches her eyebrows, waiting.

I close my eyes and drop my head back against the pillow. "I'm in love with him," I groan.

"Told you," Claire says. I open my eyes to find her holding out a hand toward Abbi. Abbi smacks a ten-dollar bill into it.

"You bet on this?" I blurt out.

"Obviously," Abbi laughs.

"Hey, I wanted in!" Vivi announces.

Chloe shifts closer to me. "He's in love with you too, Sofia."

"I know," I whisper. "But right now—"

"You don't need to explain yourself," Abbi interrupts me, holding up a hand. "Just know that no matter what, Theo's got your back. And so do we. Focus on the surgery, on healing. But whatever you need, we're all here."

I smile at my little girl group, unbelievably grateful that I've connected with them in such a short amount of time.

A knock on my bedroom door draws my attention.

"I hope you know that means me too," Margaret Lawrence says.

Tears prick the corners of my eyes, and I blink rapidly, trying to hold them back. What is she doing here? Doesn't she hate me? Isn't she angry with Theo for pulling strings on my behalf?

"Can I come in?" Margaret asks.

The girls immediately make room for her as I nod, holding out a hand.

Margaret shifts closer to me and takes my hand in hers as Chloe slips out of the chair so Margaret can sit down.

"I didn't know—" I start, nearly sobbing.

"Shh," she hushes me, her tone gentle. "Of course you didn't."

"But now—"

"Now you are a beautiful woman who my son cares deeply about. From the moment I met you, I knew you were special. Regardless of your feelings for or relationship with Theo, it would be an honor to help you navigate the labyrinth that is healthcare in our country. It's not fair, sometimes it's not right, and it's very rarely easy, but Lance and I have spent years funding research initiatives that will hopefully help produce cures for many illnesses plaguing the world today. Through our work, we have built relationships and connections with doctors and hospitals throughout the country. If I can leverage any of those to better support you, I'm going to do it."

I hear one of the girls suck in a deep breath. It's so quiet that the silence pulses in my eardrums.

"But my dad—" I try again, catching Chloe's frown.

"Did what a lot of parents who feel desperate would have done," Margaret explains.

I close my eyes and squeeze her fingers. "I don't know how to do this part."

"Accept support?" she laughs lightly, turning to look at my friends. "You're doing an okay job, Sofia. You need to understand that the people who show up do it because they want to. It's not out of obligation. You don't need to feel guilty for having people in your life who care about you, some so much that they'll do anything to help." She lifts an eyebrow and I know she's hinting at my dad.

I manage to nod as my emotions surge forward. My blinking increases and I work a swallow, trying to get a handle on all the feelings swimming around.

"I had the pleasure of meeting your dad," Margaret continues, flashing me a smile. "He's lovely. I hope when you're recovered and feeling better we can have a dinner together. Maybe at Theo's? That way it can be comfortable and laid-back, more like a family gathering."

I roll my lips together and nod. "I'd really like that, Margaret."

"Me too."

"The game's starting," Claire announces.

We all settle into our chairs and watch as the Hawks take the ice. When Theo's name is called, I smile. I miss him immensely. What a privilege it is to watch him live his passion and play the game of his heart.

What a special moment to do so with his mom at my side.

What a beautiful now I'm living. I squeeze my eyes closed for a second and silently wish that I experience more nows as special as this one.

CHAPTER 25
THEO

The Hawks are off to a solid season with three wins under our belt but the only thing I care about as I step off the plane in Boston is getting to Mass General.

"Want to ride together?" Jesse asks me and I nod, recognizing his thoughtfulness. His sister may be pushing me away, but he knows how badly I want to be in the waiting room, hearing the updates as they occur.

Plus, my mom went to visit Sofia two nights ago. After their chat, I received a text from Sofia that offered a glimmer of hope.

SOFIA

> I need to get through this surgery. But then I want to talk. I miss you, Theo.

She didn't pick up when I called, and Jesse mentioned that she's been bombarded with visitors from her family as well as the BHH girls, so I didn't take it personally.

But now that the game is behind me and I'm back in Boston, all I want is to be closer to my girl.

Jesse and I ride the team bus back to The Meadows and walk over to my car.

"Hey!" Yaeger calls out.

I turn.

"What do you need?" he asks.

"We'll send food," Austin assures us.

"Or shots," Panda jokes but I can tell he's distressed about Sofia.

"We'll keep you posted on what's happening," I reply.

The guys nod. Jesse waves his hand in thanks.

Then, Jesse and I drive to the hospital in silence, both of us praying for a positive outcome for the woman we can't live without.

"IT WENT WELL. NO SURPRISES." Mom shakes my shoulder, waking me.

I bolt upright in the hospital chair, nearly sending Mom flying. I grab her arm to keep her from stumbling back. "Sorry," I clear my throat. "It's done?"

Mom nods, tears in her eyes. "It's done. She's in the post-anesthesia care unit recovering. They'll keep her there overnight before moving her to her own room."

"Can I see her?"

Mom nods again. "She's asking for you."

I jump to my feet, shaking the cobwebs of sleep from my mind. Guilt sweeps through me for falling asleep in the first place but when I glance around the waiting room, I note Jesse's mom waking him as well. The past few days have been rough, being away from Sofia and Boston, having to play hockey when my mind never left this hospital.

I flip my chin to Jesse, and he nods. His mom gives me a tearful smile and gestures toward the hallway that will take me to Sofia. A nurse leads me to the care unit and indicates the bed Sofia is lying in.

When she spots me, she smiles, stretching the thin tube of oxygen that rests on her upper lip. Her legs are sheathed in compression boots, her hair in a messy bun on top of her head, and still, she's the most beautiful woman I've ever laid eyes on.

"We only have five minutes," she murmurs, her voice raspy.

"I love you so much," I blurt out, tears springing to my eyes as I drop to her bedside.

Her fingers find my hair as I rest my head against her shoulder, kissing her jawline.

"How do you feel?" I ask.

"The pain meds are a godsend." She shifts so I can see her eyes. "Thank you for waiting all day, even when I said I didn't want you to."

"I'm not usually one to press but this time, it was pure selfishness. I needed to be here for me as much as for you."

"I'm glad you stayed," she whispers.

"I'll always stay, Sof. I'm not going anywhere."

Her tongue swipes over her bottom lip and I sit back to grab her a glass of water. Guiding the straw to her mouth, I hold the cup steady as she takes a few small sips.

"Theo." I can tell by the look in her eyes, the seriousness of her tone, that she wants to have the big conversation now.

"We don't have to talk about this now. Baby, the only thing that matters is you getting better, feeling stronger. I'm here. When you're ready, I'll still be here."

"I love you," she forges ahead. "The way I feel about you is like nothing I've ever experienced. It's different. It's special. It means everything to me. The thought that my family hurt yours—"

"It doesn't matter."

"It does," she insists. "It matters because I want to go all in with you. I want the tomorrows and the forevers and I can't stop thinking that our past is too messy and my future too uncertain."

I pause, listening to what she's truly telling me. She's scared, she doesn't know how to navigate this, she's unsure how to have a relationship outside of the moment, and the last time she tried that, the guy let her down. "I get it," I say. "So let's take it slow."

"Slow?"

"Yeah. One day at a time, one moment at a time. We'll live in the now, address the past when necessary, and talk about the future when we want to. We don't need to dwell on it or have everything figured out. We just need this—me and you." I kiss her nose.

When I pull back, she's smiling. "You really think we can do that?"

"I think we can do anything we want if we both want it. And there's nothing more in the world I want than to be with you, Sof."

"Me too."

"Then it's settled." I lean back and push some of her hair away from her face. "I love you, Sofia Carpenter, and there isn't anything I wouldn't do for you."

"Like make sure I had the best doctors on my team?"

How the hell did she find out about that? I decide to own it because—"Anything. I will do anything."

"I love you too, Theo." My girl gives me one of those real smiles that slows everything down, even time. I revel in it, memorizing the shade of chocolate in her eyes, the curve of her lips.

"Excuse me." The nurse pops her head in. "Your time is up."

"Give him one more minute. Please," Sofia begs, still smiling at me.

The nurse holds up one finger and ducks back out.

"What else do you need to say?" I ask Sofia.

"I want a kiss." She closes her eyes and puckers her lips.

I laugh but acquiesce and brush a soft kiss over her lips. "That's a given, baby."

"And I need you to visit Sam. He's taking his exam on Thursday, and I need to know if he passes."

I chuckle but nod. "I'll visit Sam." Glancing around, I remark, "Hospitals and prisons."

Sofia smirks. "Second chances."

"Yeah, baby." I kiss her goodbye when the nurse comes to escort me out. My girl gives me one last smile, kissing two of her fingers and extending them toward me. I wave and leave the unit with a lighter heart and a clearer mind. In fact, I feel better than I have in over a week.

Because Sofia and I are a sure thing. We just need to slow down and appreciate it more.

"I'M ON DRIVING DUTIES," Chloe announces, grabbing a sheet of paper on my kitchen island and writing down her name.

"Oh, good," Claire remarks.

"You could get a car, you know?" Abbi says.

"She doesn't have one either," Claire points at Vivi.

Vivi shrugs and places her palms on her belly. "My chauffeur feels safer driving me around anyway."

Dec grins as Easton smacks the back of his head.

"How you holding up?" Austin asks me as I lean back, taking in the scene unfolding in my living room and kitchen.

"Better now that I saw Sofia," I answer honestly.

"When are they discharging her?"

"Two more days. Jesse and Sofia's parents are at the

hospital now," I add, explaining why Jesse is absent from this random gathering.

I was only home from visiting Sam to congratulate him on getting his GED for fifteen minutes when there was a knock on my door. Half the Hawks and their partners rolled through, armed with food, magazines, and curated Spotify playlists.

The guys quickly lounged around, ordering dinner. But the girls sprung into action, putting together a meal chart, a driving schedule, a cleaning service, and lists of books and audiobooks to keep Sofia entertained.

"You guys," I interrupt. All the women stop and look at me. "I think Sofia's dad is going to stay for a while, move in with her and Jesse until she gets back on her feet."

"No worries. We have a schedule for all the things." Claire holds up a notebook where a color-coded chart swims before my eyes.

"Some of this food is for you too." Chloe smiles.

Vivi pats my back. "It isn't easy traveling when the person you love is holed up in the hospital." Her eyes cut to Yaeger and that old flicker of guilt burns in my gut. But when Vivi looks up at me, she's smiling, no anger in her expression. "And if you need company, the food alone will lure any of these guys over."

I laugh. "You saying they wouldn't come just because of my charming personality?"

Vivi grins. "For Sofia, yes. For you...jury's still out."

"Hey!" I wrap an arm around Vivi's shoulders, relieved that I got back to a good place with Yaeger. The truth is, Genevieve was a big part in smoothing over that strain and now, I consider her a friend just as much as her husband.

"How are you?" she asks, lowering her voice.

"Better now that we talked."

"And?" She quirks an eyebrow.

"We're taking things...slow. One day at a time," I share.

"Best way to do it. If you plan too much, life throws you a curveball."

"Yeah," I agree, glancing around the space at my team. My friends. Last year, none of these guys knew my real name. Now, they're showing up to support my girl and have become more like family. "You're right."

"Don't I know it," Vivi remarks.

The doorbell rings and Easton heads straight for it. "The wings are here."

"You ordered wings?" Claire hollers, gesturing toward all the food the girls brought over.

"We're playing Xbox too!" Panda holds up a controller.

Claire wrinkles her nose. "I can't wait until Sofia's home."

"Tell me about it," Abbi agrees.

I smile, grateful that these people, my chosen family, have also chosen the woman who owns my heart: Sofia Carpenter.

CHAPTER 26
SOFIA

"You sure this isn't going to be awkward?" I ask Theo as I fix the last place setting on the dining table.

He looks up from tossing the salad on the kitchen island. "I never said that."

"What?"

"Of course it's going to be awkward." He shrugs, like it's no big deal that his parents and my parents, Dad included, are getting together for dinner tonight.

"I brought popcorn," my brother announces, right on cue. Jesse strides into Theo's kitchen with a massive grin, and an even bigger bag of SkinnyPop in hand.

Theo wrinkles his nose. "You couldn't get real popcorn? With butter?"

Jesse shakes the bag. "It has pink Himalayan salt."

Theo pretends to gag.

Jesse shakes his head and opens the bag, sliding onto a barstool. "For a fancy kid who's supposed to have pedigree, I question your food choices."

Theo rolls his eyes and shows Jesse the salad he made, brimming with pears, walnuts, and blue cheese. "You'll take that back when you try this."

"Salad," Jesse scoffs.

"Guys!" I clap my hands, redirecting their attention to the matter at hand. "Margaret, Lance, Mom, Mitch, and Dad are coming for dinner. To sit, together, around this table." I gesture to the table, beautifully done with formal place settings. Not going to lie, I impressed myself with how pretty it looks. Sure, I copied a Pinterest photo, but it looks exactly like the pin!

"Great job on the linen napkins, Sofia," Jesse comments.

"Thanks. I'm pretty proud of myself," I say. "But I'm also stressed about dinner. What if—"

"A fight breaks out?" Jesse tosses a handful of popcorn into his mouth.

"Ted and Mitch get into it?" Theo wonders.

"Your mom hates the salad?" Jesse asks.

Theo frowns and peeks at his salad.

I roll my eyes, about to voice the fears swimming in my head—mainly, what if we all get stuck on a conversation about the past and the entire evening is ruined—when a knock sounds on the door.

"Oh my God! They're here." I wring my hands and shoot Theo a pleading look.

"Early too," Jesse comments, not bothering to put down the popcorn.

I stride to the door and pull it open, shuffling back a step. "Heather!" I exclaim, pulling my favorite bride into a hug.

"I'm so happy to see you!" she gushes, hugging me back.

"Hey, Sofia." Preston hugs me next.

"What are you doing here?" I blurt out. "Not that I'm not thrilled it's just, this is such a surprise!" I step back so they can enter Theo's apartment.

Theo's smiling hard as he welcomes his brother and sister-in-law.

"Let me guess." Jesse stands and extends a hand to Preston. "Came for the entertainment."

Preston laughs. "Sure did. Preston."

"Jesse. Good to meet you."

"Hi." Heather waves. "I'm Heather. And I hate to disappoint you all, but the parents are going to be late."

"What?" I ask, immediately concerned.

Heather pulls out her phone and shows me an image on the screen. "Yeah," she explains. "Margaret just sent me this. Apparently, they all met up for a drink at this little wine bar Margaret and Lance discovered…"

Jesse guffaws. "They're pregaming?"

My eyes widen as I take in the photo. Rosy cheeks, big smiles, huddled close together. "My dad has his arm around your mom." I look up at Theo.

While I'm in a state of shock, he's obviously pleased. "This is great!"

"Epic," Jesse agrees.

"They invited us but…" Heather wrinkles her nose. "I wanted to see you," she whispers to me. "Preston, can you pour us some wine?" Heather leads me to the living room.

"Now you can relax and chat," Theo says, whole-heartedly on board with this turn of events.

Preston pours two wineglasses and brings them to Heather and me. "Relax." He winks at me. "The parents got this covered. In fact, I think they actually like each other."

"Wow," I breathe out. "I didn't see this coming."

"Isn't that great? Finally, a good curveball," Heather remarks.

Months ago, I helped plan her wedding in Maui before drunkenly sleeping with her brother-in-law. Now, we're hanging out in Boston, I'm recovering from surgery, and my parents, Dad included, have forged a social connection with Theo's. The past few months have tossed a lot of curveballs my way but Heather's right, this is definitely a good one.

"Cheers!" She holds up her wine and I clink my glass against hers.

"How was Italy?" I ask, a little in love with the fact that Preston and Heather's honeymoon was a three-month vacation.

"Ooh, it was beautiful. You and Theo have to join us the next time we go to Santa Margherita Ligure. That place is truly life changing," she says, telling me all about the picturesque Italian seaside.

Jesse catches my eye and winks, knowing that I'm still processing how this, these people in this place, all together and happy, has become my now.

The guys come over with drinks and we sit around the living room, talking and catching up. I settle back against Theo's chest, listening to everyone's funny stories and travel experiences. An hour ago, I was a nervous wreck, trying to plan for every disaster that could befall our dinner party.

But now, I'm relaxed. Our parents are still MIA, sipping wine. Preston and Heather showed up unannounced. We're already two bottles of wine in. And I've never felt more at peace.

I smile to myself. I got my wish, more beautiful, special, memorable nows.

"You okay?" Theo whispers in my ear.

I tip my head back and smile. "I'm great. I love you."

"Love you more, Sof. No bullshit."

EPILOGUE

THEO

Seven Years Later

"You're doing great!" Sofia squeezes our surrogate's hand as she births our second child into the world. "You're incredible and you got this."

Jenna gives one last push and then the most beautiful crying I've ever heard pierces the delivery room.

"Congratulations!" the doctor announces, pulling me forward. A nurse hands me a pair of scissors as the doctor holds the umbilical cord taut. "It's a girl!"

While the buzz in the delivery room is loud, all sound ceases for an instant. The weight of the scissors in my hand is heavy as I cut the cord. Then, sound comes rushing forward as I catch my first glimpse of my daughter.

Sofia hugs Jenna, the two of them crying together. My emotions are all over the place as I stare at my daughter for the first time. Her face is wrinkly, her eyes screwed closed, and man, does she have a set of lungs on her. "She's perfect."

"She is," the nurse agrees, handing her to Sofia who is already seated at Jenna's bedside, just in a bra, ready for some skin-to-skin contact.

"What's her name?" the nurse asks as I take the seat beside my wife.

"Jenna," Sofia murmurs and I nod.

"Jenna Margaret," I say.

Our surrogate Jenna looks up from the bed, tears streaming down her face.

"Thank you for everything." My voice shakes. "You've given us the most incredible gift."

"You have a beautiful family," she responds with pure sincerity. "And Dexter is going to be thrilled that she's a girl."

We all laugh because our four-year-old son was adamant that he wants a sister. While Sofia was able to carry Dexter to term, she suffered a handful of miscarriages afterward. Eventually, we decided to try the surrogate route and have been granted a true miracle through Jenna. The moment we met her, Sofia said, "she's the one," and now, she's part of our growing family too.

I run my finger along baby Jenna's shoulder as her howling dies down and her eyes close, heavy with sleep. "I'm in love with her already."

"So am I," Sofia whispers. Her tear-filled eyes meet mine and hold. "How lucky are we?"

"The luckiest," I agree, knowing how blessed we are.

While the past few years haven't been easy, they've been filled with moments of incomparable beauty. We formed a family in Boston with the Hawks, and our parents and siblings created a new type of family, centered around our love and Dexter, that goes beyond any support system we could have dreamed up. While we suffered losses, we've also experienced great joys through our friendships, Sam included, and loved ones.

"Dexter's waiting for an update," one of the nurses informs us.

"I better go fill him in. I'm sure our parents and Jesse, Preston, and Heather are just as desperate for the news." I kiss Sofia's cheek. Our family has been in the waiting room since the moment Sofia and I arrived to support Jenna.

Not wanting to miss a moment, I pop into the waiting room on a wave of excitement. Our parents and siblings look up expectantly but my gaze is trained on Dexter.

"Girl?" he asks hopefully.

"Girl," I confirm.

Our family's cheers ring out and my little guy rushes me, wrapping his arms around my legs for a second before I swing him up into my arms. I look at Mom and Dad, Sofia's parents, Preston, Heather, and Jesse, and smile. "Jenna Margaret is here and she's perfect. Sofia and Jenna are great too."

Mom clasps her hands over her heart, tears welling in her eyes. Her and Sofia's mom hug, both of them crying, before wrapping Dexter and me in their arms. Dad shakes my hand followed by Ted and Mitch. Preston and Jesse wish me congratulations and Heather kisses my cheek, her face beaming.

"Go meet your sissy, Dex," she says.

I nod in thanks and extricate us from the group, rushing back to the hospital room with Dexter.

Before we enter, my little dude steels his shoulders and takes a deep breath. I push open the door and his eyes zero in on his sister, the most awe filled expression crossing his face. I move him closer to Sofia and she angles baby Jenna so Dexter can see her face.

"Hi little baby," he whispers, his voice suddenly sounding older than it did yesterday. "I'm your big brother. Dexter. I'm going to read you books and show you how to race cars and teach you to ride a bike, okay?"

Baby Jenna sighs, her eyes closed, her body curled into a ball. Dexter reaches out to touch her cheek and Sofia catches my eye, hers filled with pure love.

I wrap my arms around Sofia, Dexter, and baby Jenna,

holding my family close. I never thought I'd marry or start a family, but when I went all in with Sofia, my entire outlook changed. Suddenly, I knew there was no future but one with her. I adopted a worldview like Preston's and stopped seeing him as the better Lawrence. Instead, we just became the Lawrence brothers.

While hockey keeps me busy, my schedule wrought with travel, my family keeps me grounded. Now, there's a new little princess to rule my heart and I couldn't be happier.

Sofia squeezes Dexter's hand. "You're already the best big brother, Dex." She drops a kiss to Jenna's head and murmurs, "To my brave little girl, may your days be filled with moments, and magic, and miracles."

I smile, taking in the heartfelt moment, knowing just how difficult it's been for Sofia to get to this point, to arrive at this day, to fully embrace this now.

I spend a breath soaking up the second, memorizing this feeling, reveling in this high. It's so spectacular, it's everything.

And I wouldn't trade it for the world. Because I already have the world, right here in this hospital room, where miracles are made.

THANK you for reading Theo and Sofia's emotional story! Want more Hawks? Don't miss Scott Reland's swoony attempt to win the heart of his rival's daughter in The Score Keeper, releasing March 3!

HEY READER!

Hey there reader!

Thanks so much for reading *The Hustler*! I hope you loved this redemption story and enjoyed seeing Theo grow through Sofia's love.

If you'd like to pass along your thoughts on this book, I'd love it if you would please leave a review. Make sure you preorder the final book in the BHH series, The Score Keeper, coming March 3!

To be in the know about book news, please subscribe to my monthly newsletter. Or, come hang out in my Facebook Reader Group, Gina Azzi's Book Besties.

Thank you so much for all the BHH love! It means the world to me!

XO,
   Gina

ALSO BY GINA AZZI

Knoxville Coyotes Football:

Faked and Fumbled

Surprised and Sacked

Trapped and Tackled

The Burnt Clovers Trilogy:

Rebellious Rockstar

Resentful Rockstar

Restless Rockstar

Tennessee Thunderbolts:

Hot Shot's Mistake

Brawler's Weakness

Rookie's Regret

Playboy's Reward

Hero's Risk

Bad Boy's Downfall

Lock 'Em Down

Boston Hawks Hockey:

The Sweet Talker

The Risk Taker

The Faker

The Rule Maker

The Defender

The Heart Chaser

The Trailblazer

The Hustler

The Score Keeper

Second Chance Chicago Series:

Broken Lies

Twisted Truths

Saving My Soul

Healing My Heart

The Kane Brothers Series:

Rescuing Broken (Jax's Story)

Recovering Beauty (Carter's Story)

Reclaiming Brave (Denver's Story)

My Christmas Wish

(A Kane Family Christmas

+ *One Last Chance* FREE prequel)

Finding Love in Scotland Series:

My Christmas Wish

(A Kane Family Christmas

+ *One Last Chance* FREE prequel)

One Last Chance (Daisy and Finn)

This Time Around (Aaron and Everly)

One Great Love

The College Pact Series:

The Last First Game (Lila's Story)

Kiss Me Goodnight in Rome (Mia's Story)

All the While (Maura's Story)

Me + You (Emma's Story)

Standalone

Corner of Ocean and Bay

www.ingramcontent.com/pod-product-compliance
Lightning Source LLC
Chambersburg PA
CBHW032158190726
48289CB00007BA/2285